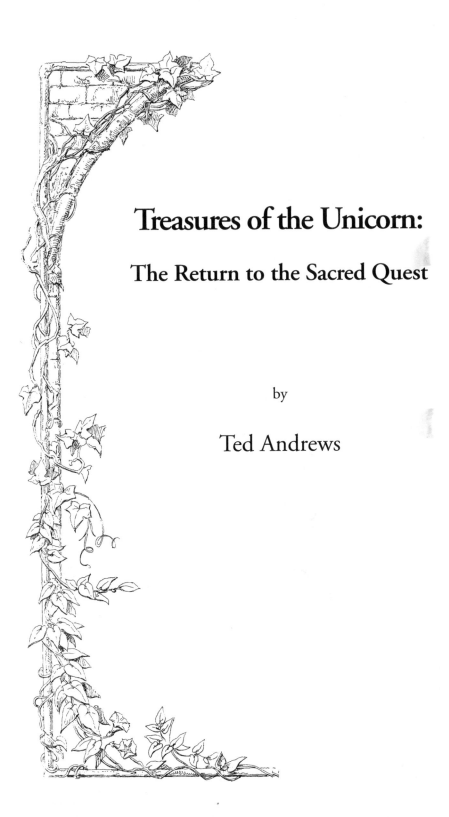

Treasures of the Unicorn:

The Return to the Sacred Quest

by

Ted Andrews

Dedication

To Kodi and Cheyenne with great love.
You are forever in our hearts!

Forthcoming Titles by Ted Andrews

He Always Wanted to…

More Simplified Magic

Psychic Protection

Spirit Masks & the Art of Shapeshifting

Dragon

The Magical Name (revised edition)

Music Therapy (A pocket Guide Book from Crossing Press)

Music and Spoken Audio by Ted Andrews

Roses of Light

Upon the Wings of Angels

Mystery of the Fire Spirits

Uncover Your Past Lives

Psychic Protection

Discover Your Spirit Animal

Enchantment of the Faerie Realm (forthcoming)

Entering the Tree of Life (forthcoming)

Developing Psychic Touch (forthcoming)

Other Books by Ted Andrews through Llewellyn Publications

Simplified Magic

Sacred Power in Your Name

How to See and Read the Aura

Dream Alchemy

How to Uncover Your Past Lives

Sacred Sounds

How to Meet and Work with Spirit Guides

How to Heal with Color

Magickal Dance

Enchantment of the Faerie Realm

The Occult Christ: Angelic Mysteries & the Divine Feminine

Animal-Speak

The Healer's Manual

How to Develop and Use Psychometry

Crystal Balls & Crystal Bowls

TABLE OF CONTENTS

Introduction: The Unicorn Prophecy   2

Chapter 1:   The Wonders of the Unicorn   10
              Exercise 1: The Unicorn Journal   18

Chapter 2:   Sacred Secrets   22
              Exercise 2: Preparing for the Unicorn Quest   40

Chapter 3:   The Alicorn's Magic   46
              Exercise 3: Dance of the Unicorn   58
              Exercise 4: The Wondrous Horn   66

Chapter 4:   The Eastern Unicorn   76
              Exercise 5: Dances of the Sacred Beasts   86
              Exercise 6: Council of Imaginary Beasts   92
              Exercise 7: Ghenghis Khan and the Unicorn   98

Chapter 5:   The Lion and the Unicorn   104
              Exercise 8: The Lady and the Unicorn   118
              Exercise 9: The Sacred Shield of the Unicorn   122
              Exercise 10: The Hunt of the Unicorn   132

Chapter 6:   The Unicorn and Christ   142
              Exercise 11: The Holy Quest   152

Chapter 7:   The Unicorn's Companions   162
              Exercise 12: The Unicorn Boy   180

Chapter 8:   The Alchemical Mysteries   190
              Exercise 13: Sacred Sex and the Sacred Beasts   210
              Exercise 14: The Unicorn and the Wood Nymph   218

Conclusion: The Sacred Quest of the Unicorn   226

Bibliography   236

Index   239

LIST OF ILLUSTRATIONS

Fairy and Unicorn   9

A Family of Unicorns   39

Unicorns in Moonlight   75

The Unicorn Tapestries

   The Start of the Hunt   110

   The Unicorn Rids the Stream of Poison   111

   The Unicorn Leaps the Stream   112

   The Unicorn Defends Itself   113

   The Unicorn is Tamed by the Maiden   114

   The Unicorn is Killed and Brought to the Castle 115

   The Unicorn in Captivity   116

Madonna and the Unicorn   148

The Annunciation   150

Unicorn with Women   204

Unicorn with Maiden   217

Untitled   235

INTRODUCTION

The Unicorn Prophecy

It was a secret with great power and great magic.

It was a secret that would forever help me to remember.

It would forever remind me to believe.

*It would forever teach me that wonder is as necessary to life
as the very air we breathe and the food we eat.*

My entrance into the woods in the early morning was always heralded by the soft cooing of the morning dove and the whistle of the bob white. These were always special times, so it was a greeting I would become very familiar with during my childhood. On two of those occasions, I would encounter something so special, so magnificent, that only now am I able to speak of it!

Behind our house was a creek separating the woods from our backyard. The woods were dotted with pockets of clearings that were fun to seek out, each one as a secret world filled with hidden treasures to be uncovered.

Beyond one small clearing was the pond. At night the pond was alive with the voices of frogs, but in the early morning they were comparatively quiet. Walking the edge of the pond, the stillness of the water was always broken by the splashing of frogs scattering into the water to avoid footsteps. Dragonflies danced about like flying rainbows.

On the far side of the pond was a fallen sassafras tree with most of its roots still in the ground. Until the pond was filled by bulldozers and the surrounding woods cut to build new houses, it was a favorite place for solitude. I would sit at the base of the tree, watching the dragonflies race and soar about. Occasionally I would snap a small branch from the sassafras tree and inhale its wonderful fragrance. To this day, the smell of sassafras transports me back to that time and place.

In the spring, just a year or two after my family moved to this area, I arose early on a Saturday morning. As I stepped out the front door, I heard the morning dove and the bob white greet me. Even though I knew that I could not be seen from the woods, the child within me—with that instinctual wisdom that resides in every child—knew that both the dove and the bob white were well aware that I had stepped out of my house.

The air was sweet on mornings like this, and being an asthmatic child, it was much the sweeter. I would take a moment or two and deeply inhale the freshness, feeling the air alive within my lungs. The moon was faint but still visible in the morning sky. The dew glistened heavily upon the grass.

Introduction

Jumping off the front porch, I angled across the side yard toward the woods. As I reached the creek, I glanced back across the yard and grinned, seeing my footprints clearly in the wet grass. Already the dew was soaking through my shoes and socks, making me feel that much more alive. I imagined the dew was a special elixir the grasses had given just to me. Sometimes that elixir could make me fly; other times it would enable me to become a deer or a wolf. It could help me do or become whatever my heart fancied at the time. And what better place was there to act it out than in the woods.

I leaped, tip-toe style, across the creek to keep from getting my feet any wetter, using the stones from a dam my brothers and I had built some time ago. I avoided the heavier, taller weeds on the opposite side, following the creek bed for a little ways, cutting across the weeds toward the pond. I headed for a path that would less likely further soak my shoes. Not that it would do any good. Already I could hear them squishing. I considered the squishing a magical sound—the song the dew sang to tell me its magic was being awakened for me.

The earth beneath my feet was damp and springy, making me feel as if I were light enough to bounce to the pond. Approaching the pond, I knelt down at its edge, peering for frogs hiding there. On days like these, I'd try to catch one, but I never succeeded. I'm not sure I ever truly wanted to. Even though I had held frogs before, they felt funny to me, and I always believed my brothers and friends suspected my uncomfortableness. I wasn't about to let them know for sure, giving them fuel for teasing me. That I was only seven or eight years old would be no excuse. I half-heartedly convinced myself that if I could catch one, it would prove I was just as brave as they were, then I wouldn't have to worry about being teased.

On this day I didn't even feign catching frogs. I just looked at them. To my surprise, the frogs seemed to be looking back at me. Their big round eyes held me fixed, and in that moment, it no longer mattered if I ever caught one again. I straightened up, puzzled by the feeling, but just like a kid, brushed it aside, accepting it. I walked around the edge of the pond toward the sassafras tree, and perched myself upon its bent trunk, wedging between several of the larger branches. I leaned back against the trunk of a smaller tree that had grown, up against my sassafras perch. This arrangement suited my small frame. My feet dangled, toes barely brushing the top of the overgrown grasses beneath them.

The morning dove and bob white had stopped their daily greetings. Even the dragonflies were quiet in their flight. With my eyes were half closed, I enjoyed the morning quiet. The only sounds were my breathing and the rustling of my jeans when I moved.

A breeze brushed softly across me, and I heard a faint tinkling sound, like tiny bells being shaken. I sat up, tilting my head slightly, listening a little more intently, but the sound had faded when I moved. I shifted a little, telling myself it was the wind playing tricks on me and I leaned back once more.

Then there was a rustling of weeds on the opposite side of the pond. At first I thought it was just someone else who had gotten up early to enjoy the morning by the pond. I peered across the pond, trying to peek through the tall weeds and trees and caught a glimpse of a pair of hooved legs! My heart jumped and I held my breath, trying not to move at all. Although deer frequented the area, it was unusual to ever see them up close. Deer had to be caught by surprise. I tried to contain my excitement, thinking I was about to become very lucky. Watching the shadowed form move silently through the weeds, I smiled. Finally I'd get to see a deer up close!

I didn't blink. I didn't breathe for what seemed an eternity. All I could see was a faint form through the tall weeds. It froze, holding perfectly still, just beyond my sight. I could make out what I thought was a head tilting slightly, as if listening before stepping into the open at the pond's edge. I held my breath, sure that the beating of my heart would give my presence away and send the deer back into the woods without an actual appearance.

The weeds rustled softly and the faint tinkling of bells sounded again. It stepped out to the pond's edge. I gasped. My eyes widened. It was not a deer that stepped from the tall weeds. It was a magnificent unicorn! It turned its head toward me at the sound of the my gasp and held me fixed with its sparkling, blue eyes. I didn't move. I didn't blink. I didn't even breathe. I just stared, wide eyed. In that moment a soft breeze brushed across me, carrying the fragrance of apple blossoms. This time I could distinctly hear the tinkling of the bells. A soft, tiny chiming brushed over me as if the breeze itself carried invisible bells within it.

The unicorn stood frozen at the edge of the pond directly across from me. Its eyes were so expressive I was almost certain it recognized me. Some distant part of me knew I was not to speak or move.

The horn stood strong in the center of the unicorn's head and had what seemed a spiral marking, shimmering with a silver tint in the early morning light. The unicorn's coat seemed to shift in color and brilliance, depending upon how it caught the light, sometimes white, sometimes silver. A soft haze surrounded the animal.

Keeping its eyes fixed upon me, the unicorn bent its front legs, and lowered the horn to the surface of the pond. As the point touched the pond's surface, I heard the soft tinkling of the bells again and the haunting, sweet song of a young girl singing in the distance. The surface of the water bubbled like it was being brought to a boil and ripples spread outward from the unicorn's horn tip. The fragrance of the trees and weeds nearby grew stronger and clearer. The smell of sassafras swirled around me, as if being freed from the tree itself. Hundreds of dragon flies began to circle, their iridescent wings reflecting a multitude of colors dancing in the air.

As the unicorn raised its horn tip from the water, stillness fell over the pond once more. Its eyes continued to hold mine. Tilting its head slightly, I am sure the unicorn smiled. Before I could blink or respond in any way, it turned and vanished once more through the weeds and into the woods beyond. I do not know how long it was before I moved, but it was not until a dragonfly lighted upon my arm.

I left my perch and moved slowly around the edge of the pond to where I had seen the unicorn. All that remained of its presence was half of a hoof print and several weeds bent but unbroken. I watched as they rose to their former straight position. I cocked my head every which way, listening. There was no sound. There was no sign.

I knew no one would believe me, but it didn't matter. I didn't plan to tell a soul. Something in the unicorn's eyes told me this was secret. This was special. This was not the time to tell. The telling would come later. A part of me knew this, accepting without understanding. For the time being, I would hold the encounter close and treasure it in my own heart, knowing it would be revealed only when the unicorn permitted.

Looking back now, I know that this was when I experienced how tangible the sacred could feel and be. At the time, there was nothing to which I could relate the experience—no dream and no church experience. Nothing. It was new. It was strange. It was all-encompassing. It filled me with such an intensity of wonder and awe so strong and so powerful that even today, when I think upon it, my heart jumps and I hear my blood roaring new life through my body.

At the same time, there comes with this memory a tremendous sense of calmness. Something was being awakened in me. Or born. From that day on I knew the reality of miracles. Beyond myth. Beyond fantasy. Beyond promise. From that day forward, a part of me would always know dreams are never lost—only forgotten.

I did not know it at the time, but mine were only just beginning....

Skeptics will say the unicorn should not to be taken literally. Humans can be very smug. There will always be those who see the unicorn as "the stuff of fiction." Some will always view the unicorn as only a product of the imagination since no scientific data records its presence. Nonetheless, when we lose our ability to see as a child sees, the world becomes a place of fear rather than a place of wonder and enchantment.

INTRODUCTION

It is not the purpose of this book to prove the existence of the unicorn or the reality of my own experiences with this marvelous creature. Rarely does the scientific community accept anecdotal evidence. The experiences of others, however, even when anecdotal, provide a barometer for others to measure their own experiences. These experiences can provide a map for others in their own search. And search is what each of us must do.

The purpose of this book is to show how we can open ourselves to the mysteries of the unicorn—its essence and its magic—whether we look upon it as a literal creature or an archetype. The purpose of this book is to help readers find the eyes of the child once more. Whether we view the unicorn as reality or symbol, it has the power to heal, bless, and transform, opening even the most tightly closed hearts. By opening ourselves, first to its possibility and then to its actuality, we reawaken our sense of wonder and delight in ourselves and the world. This is the first of many treasures of the unicorn.

> *Now I will believe that there are unicorns!*
> William Shakespeare, "The Tempest," iii, 3.

The unicorn is the true prophecy of paradox. Its reality is hard to define and difficult to deny. While many may claim the unicorn as their own, none can capture it. Knowledge of the unicorn is something you keep close to the heart, even while you give it away. With this knowledge, you can take the old and express it anew.

The unicorn must be honored and treasured or its virtue is lost. It will lead you to the higher path, and yet show you where you must follow your own path. Although the unicorn's message is for all, we each must find our own understanding of it.

When we find the treasures of the unicorn, we find the treasures within ourselves!

Fairy and Unicorn

CHAPTER 1

The Wonders of the Unicorn

*Alice could not help her lips curling up
into a smile as she began.
"Do you know I always thought
unicorns were fabulous monsters, too.
I never saw one alive before!
"Well, now we have seen each other,"
said the Unicorn. "If you'll believe in me,
I'll believe in you. Is that a bargain?"*

Lewis Carroll
Through the Looking Glass
p. 86

The Wonders of the Unicorn

Since the earliest of times, the unicorn has mystified humans. A creature of extraordinary perception, stamina and magic, the unicorn has been a symbol of gentleness, power and fertility. It has been revered for its ability to heal and feared for its ability to kill. Within the minds and hearts of humans, its appeal has never faded for any great length of time.

Today most people see the unicorn as a horse with a horn, but its appearance and qualities have been described in a variety of ways around the world. It has been confused with the antelope, the goat, the rhinoceros and the oryx. Unicorns have been depicted as having white bodies and red heads, with horns varying from silver to rainbow hues. They have been described with having elephant's feet and as having hooves that are cloven, split, or even heart shaped. Sometimes they have a silky beard and sometimes not. Sometimes they fly—with or without wings. Some are fierce, while others embody gentleness. Some unicorns walk so softly that they merely bend the grasses they walk upon—doing no harm to them. They can roar loudly or whisper sounds like the soft tinkling of bells. No matter how they are described, they never fail to capture our imagination.

Although not as ancient in myth and lore as the dragon, the unicorn has touched all the corners of the world. Like the dragon, it has had a myriad of fanciful depictions and variations and always stir the imagination. Even today, unicorns fill people with wonder. They appear on T-shirts, mugs, paintings, and all types of merchandising. Unicorns have become the models for rocking horses, carousels, and cartoons.

Unicorns fascinate us because more than any other creature, mythical or imagined, they seem the most plausible. While most people believe the dragon is pure myth and fantasy, this same belief does not hold true for the unicorn. It has such close resemblance to so many animals in existence that to the average person, its reality is a possibility. The unicorn is most often depicted as related to the horse, and it has been linked to many horned creatures, usually the deer and the goat. It has also been related to the narwhal and the rhinoceros. One hundred and twenty million years ago there was even a dinosaur unicorn, the monoclonius.

CHAPTER 1

Although endowed with unusual and often magical properties through the ages, it is the unicorn's resemblance to familiar animals in nature that raises many of the doubts, casting shadows upon its being a mere fanciful creation. These similarities to known animals fuel our fascination and raise a multitude of questions:

- Could there have been such an animal?
- If the unicorn's existence is possible, could its amazing qualities be possible as well?
- Could such an animal still exist, and if so, what is it really like?
- What strange qualities does it really have?
- Can its horn truly heal?
- What common threads run through unicorn teachings around the world?
- Even if only an archetypal symbol, what can that symbol teach us?
- Is there a true unicorn treasure?
- Where is the unicorn found?
- How do we begin the search?

When we study what has been spoken and written about unicorns throughout the ages, we find common threads. When this phenomenon of "common threads" occurs in societies that have had no contact with each other, it should make little bells go off. It says we have something magnificent going on. Something wonderful and universal—something we should be paying attention to!

In ancient China, a unicorn would appear at the time of a benevolent reign or in the dreams of a mother who would give birth to a special child. As we will see later, the mother of Confucius was one such individual. Its appearance always foretold good fortune and happiness.

In India, the unicorn appeared in the epic tale *The Mahabharata* (circa 200 B.C.). In Persia, the *karkadann*, or unicorn, was ferocious and powerful enough to kill an elephant, and yet it could be tamed by the soft song of the ringdove. Alexander the Great is believed to have ridden upon a unicorn (probably related to the karkadann) by the name of Bucephalus.

The Greek historian Ctesius wrote of the unicorn in his bestiary. Aristotle spoke of two types of unicorns. Julius Caesar in his *Conquest of Gaul* told of unicorns living in the Hycernian Forest of Germany. Other Greek and Roman writers spoke of unicorns as well, including Pliny, Physiologus, and Aelian.

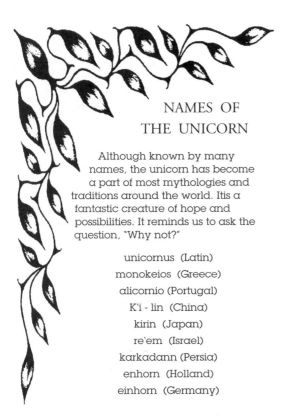

NAMES OF THE UNICORN

Although known by many names, the unicorn has become a part of most mythologies and traditions around the world. It is a fantastic creature of hope and possibilities. It reminds us to ask the question, "Why not?"

unicornus (Latin)
monokeios (Greece)
alicornio (Portugal)
K'i - lin (China)
kirin (Japan)
re'em (Israel)
karkadann (Persia)
enhorn (Holland)
einhorn (Germany)

Marco Polo was one of the first explorers to report about the unicorn, but by the 16th century, the unicorn was known throughout Europe. King John II of Portugal spoke of the unicorn, but with Christian overtones, although the unicorn was always a sign of good fortune and healing. The Middle Ages and Renaissance saw a rise in the unicorn's popularity, and today it still has ties to the history of both Scotland and England.

Reports of the unicorn's appearance in America have also occurred. In the 16th century, it was reported in Florida, along with reports of tigers and lions. In the 17th century, Dr. Olfert Dapper in northern Maine reported unicorns along the Canadian border.[1]

---

[1] J.L. Schrader, *A Medieval Bestiary* (New York: Metropolitan Museum of Art, 1986), p. 134.

Chapter 1

Around the world, the unicorn has been treated both as a natural phenomenon and as a sacred symbol. It has been called by many names,

---

BESTIARIES OF THE WORLD

Historial Animalium
by Aristotle

Historia Naturalis
by Pliny the Elder

Phyusiolgus
by Physiologus

Hexaemeron
by Saint Ambrose

Etymologiae
by Hrabanus Maurius

De Bestiis et Aliis Rebas
by Hugh of Saint Victor

Aviarium Bestiarius
by Hugo de Folieto

Bestiaire Divin
by Guilliame le Clerc

Bestiaire D'Amour
by Richard Fournivats

The Christian era of the 12th and 13th century saw a rise in the popularity of the Latin bestiaries describing the expressive power of animals. Monks, serving as copyists, often combined factual observations with allegory. Bestiaries became a fertile source of lore and information, although many of the creatures became composites of several beasts.

Some of the treatises approached the animal kingdom as a means of gaining perspective on the human condition. Monks assigned human traits to animals. In most bestiaries, the unicorn descriptions emphasized three characteristics:

- Unicorns cannot be captured.
- Unicorns have a great love for solitude.
- Unicorns have an indomitable spirit.

---

described in many bestiaries, and honored in many tales and myths. The unicorn has been associated with great figures throughout history, and its presence is found in most major religions. It is even mentioned in the Christian Bible seven times.

The question as to whether the unicorn is a natural phenomenon or a sacred symbol is difficult to resolve. The truth, as in most things, lies somewhere between. This book helps the reader to seek out the truth. I know what the truth is , but I can only provide guidelines for others seeking their own truths. Such quests are always the same, and yet each is different.

The Wonders of the Unicorn

The unicorn lives at the edges of our mind—where our more primal instincts wait to be awakened. It also lives in the real world—in special places where everything always remains a little wild and primitive. Edges and borders are places of great power and mystery, places of encounter.

This book helps the reader hear the unicorn's whisper of bells, to help the reader realize its gentle presence within the world. This book provides a starting point in seeking out the treasures of the unicorn. Think of this book as your guide to awaken and renew your sense of wonder.

Countless confidences are shared with others who open their hearts and minds to the unicorn quest. As you seek the unicorn, you will be entrusted with many secrets that will bring wonder into your life.

As you begin, remember your quest for the unicorn will occur on many levels—physical, emotional, and spiritual. As you seek out the unicorn, remember: *The unicorn must never be exploited or its magic is lost! And although it can never be tamed, it delights in the gentle pursuit!*

For those who seek, the unicorn will become more than an abstraction. You will soon realize that when a creature is chosen to symbolize an abstract principle, its characteristics demonstrate this principle in a very real way. You will remember how to believe once more. You will recall a time when you did not need practice to believe. You will grow to realize the world is still enchanted and that *the unicorn lives!*

This book guides readers to the unicorn and its many treasures. The exercises and inner seekings are simply practices in believing. They are designed to open your hearts and minds so you may once again see with your child's eyes and to feel with your child's heart, to awaken the seer within. Somewhere along the path you will meet the unicorn and your life will never be the same.

RAGGED JOHN

Tattered clothes all fluttering
Worn out voices still muttering
Ragged John comes knocking
At all the doors in town.

And when a door swings open
Then you can hear the hope in
The thin, cracked voice that wonders
If you've seen his unicorn.

And we all know John is crazy
And his mind has gone all hazy
And the only thing we really wish
Is that he just would let us be.

But John, he keeps on questing
And the poor man knows no resting
For there's something hurt within him.
And the pain won't go away.

I've heard when John was younger
He was taken with a hunger
To see the white-horned wonder
They call the unicorn.

The Wonders of the Unicorn

But when the star-horned, moon-maned dancer
Finally called, John could not answer;
Fear held him like a prisoner,
And he watched it walk away.

So now empty-eyed John hobbles
Across the village cobbles,
And the only fear he feels is
It will never come again.

Oh, when I watch old Ragged John
Go staggering by and wandering on,
I know there's nothing sadder
Than a heart that feared its dreams.

If a unicorn should call to you
Some moon-mad night all washed in dew,
Then here's the prayer to whisper:
Grant me the heart to follow.[2]

---

[2] Beatrice Farrington, *The Unicorn Treasury*, ed. Bruce Coville (New York: Doubleday, 1988), pp. 61-62. "Ragged John," copyright ©1987 by Bruce Coville and used by permission of Bruce Coville.

CHAPTER 1

The Unicorn Journal

Journaling is a powerful tool for increasing awareness of ourselves and our surroundings—both physically and spiritually. By recording your thoughts and observations, you can enhance our creativity and strengthen our clarity and commitment to our spiritual paths. As you work in your journal, you can affirm the ethereal and spiritual energies at play within your life. With something as elusive and fantastic as the unicorn, journaling becomes especially important, a sacred gift you can bestow upon yourself.

> **BENEFITS**
> - creativity
> - awareness
> - perception
> - confirming your relationship

For many, dreams—like the unicorn—elude us. Our lives seem flat and uninspired. We may have great ideas and magnificent visions, but rarely, if ever, are they actualized. By keeping a journal on the unicorn quest, you can make an investment in your own dreams and goals.

In addition to awakening and enhancing your creativity, there are many other benefits of journaling:

- recovering of your own identity,
- creating and honoring a sacred space for yourself,
- widening the realm of possibilities,
- developing a new sense of worth and power,
- strengthening your connection to your true essence, and thus to others,
- developing a place of safety and acceptance,
- nurturing of your hopes and dreams,
- remembering yourself as you once were or hoped to be, and
- gaining a greater reverence for all life.

You will need to invest time and energy in this daily task, even if only for 15 minutes. This time will become sacred. How often have you invested in the lives, hopes, dreams and plans of others? Compare this to the time you invest in yourself. Do we benefit others, if we are not true to ourselves?

There is no right or wrong way to journal. The important thing is that it be done regularly, at least every other day. You owe yourself at least that much time. Who deserves it more?

Your journal is just that—YOURS! No one else has to see it, read it, analyze it. Don't worry about capitalization or punctuation. Don't worry about complete sentences. Your journal can be whatever you wish, in whatever style you choose. Guidelines and suggestions are provided. Try them, adapt them, or even ignore them.

Do not let others hinder you in keeping your journal. Do not let moods get in the way. Do not let worry over work, kids, or spouse hinder your journal. This is part of the sacred quest. If you write in your journal regularly, you will discover your own identity and your power within it. It may be several months before you begin to recognize a new power source within you. But keep a journal!

The journal is just a tool for using one of our most powerful resources—words. Words have a great capacity to elicit change. They draw our thoughts, hopes, and wishes from that ethereal, vague mental realm and ground them in the physical. Words crystallize thoughts so they may unfold more easily and healthily within our lives.

Journals facilitate release and have many applications, especially to the sacred quest. It's OK to change your journal format! Change is positive. Change reflects growth. And you will encounter many changes on your quest.

CHAPTER 1

JOURNAL GUIDELINES

Use your journaling as part of the time you give yourself.

Use this time for yourself—no one else. Find an uninterrupted half hour to be alone. Let the significant ones in your life know this. They may try to interrupt, but be firm on this—unless there is an actual emergency. This may mean getting up a half hour earlier, or staying up a half hour later. But half an hour is the very least you should commit to everyday. It is totally FOR YOU! It is a gift and a thank you to yourself.

Design your journal the way you wish.

It may be a simple notebook or something more formal. Whatever you are comfortable with. In time, it will change anyway. You may wish to dedicate it to your quest for the unicorn and the treasures it holds for you. You may wish to make a list of the treasures you hope it has. You may wish to include a spiritual verse or a favorite story of the unicorn or anything in which you have found awe and wonder.

> *When people ask, "Why do we write morning pages?" I joke, "To get to the other side."*
>
> Julia Cameron, *The Artist's Way*, p. 12

Keep track of your unicorn encounters.

These may be in dreams, in life, in art…or anything involving the unicorn that catches your attention. You may also wish to note times in your life when your interest in unicorns was strongest. For some, this is how they begin their journaling and their unicorn quest. Others list their earliest remembrances of the unicorn, their approximate age, and important events in their life at that time and what they remember about those times.

The Wonders of the Unicorn

Leave space for periodic review.

You may wish to go back periodically and review what you have written. You may wish to add to these earlier passages as time goes by. Periodically reviewing your journal helps to reveal patterns and progress in seeking of the unicorn.

Don't limit your journal to the unicorn.

The unicorn leads us on a quest and many things occur along the way. Everything has significance, even if we do not recognize it for what it truly is. List your hopes and dreams. List your wants and desires. List what you would do if they could be fulfilled. The world of hopes and dreams, the world of possibilities, and the world of fulfillment are all part of the world of the unicorn.

Expect to find the unicorn. Write of this expectation. Trust your expectation and through your seeking, you will find the unicorn. The power of words provide a good first step in this journey. If you make the first step to seek the unicorn and its treasures, the unicorn will make a step toward you.

Most people fear searching for what may not exist. For many, there will never be any quests for the unicorn. Such a fear closes the door to a life of magic and wonder. It silences the streams and it stops the breeze.

A journal is a magickal tool. It becomes a formulary that can open doorways through caverns that lead to nether realms and wondrous adventures. But for the doors to open and the unicorn to be seen, the dream must first be spoken.

CHAPTER 2

Sacred Secrets

Herd was too ordinary a word for what they were.
Horses came in herds. And cows.

But unicorns—

there had to be special words for them all together.

Suddenly he knew what it was,
as if they had told him so in his wavery song.

He was watching a SURPRISE *of unicorns.* *

---

* Jane Yolen, "The Boy who Drew Unicorns," in *The Unicorn Treasury*, ed. Bruce Coville (New York: Doubleday, 1988), p. 161. "The Boy Who Drew Unicorns" copyright ©1987 by Jane Yolen. Used by permission of the author's agent, Curtis Brown, Ltd.

TREASURES OF THE UNICORN

The unicorn is part of the world of nature and part of the world of dreams—and completely of the heart. In many ways, it is a symbol of our longing for the mysterious and the unattainable. The search for the unicorn and its secrets is identical to the Quest for the Holy Grail—the search for our true essence and the means to express it within our lives.

The unicorn holds the knowledge of alchemy. It can stimulate healing, and its mere presence awakens purity of the heart. It holds the key to the mysteries of sexuality—physical and spiritual, teaching the strength of gentleness, curing the loss of innocence, freeing the imagination, and heralding a new beginning.

From the reaches of antiquity, the unicorn has been a relatively solitary and inaccessible creature, with most sightings of one animal and occasionally two or three. Appearing alone has added to the unicorn's mystique and contributed to our perception of it as a magickal and extraordinary creature. Despite the unicorn's elusiveness, there are ways of increasing the possibility of an actual encounter. The more we come to understand the unicorn, its behaviors, and its habitats, the more likely we are to encounter one.

Unicorns are difficult to see. They live at the edges of the mind and in the corners of the eyes. They are often sighted near waterfalls and in meadows of flowers—especially at dawn, while the dew remains upon the grass. They can also be seen during the wondrous time of twilight, as if bathing in the last sprays of sun in preparation for the moonlight dance.

The unicorn belongs to the Faerie Realm, the enchanted place of wonder that intersects with our own world at so many levels. Some say this place and all its many creatures is only imaginary, merely the "stuff of fiction." These sad statements often reflect a fear of life and its myriad wonders. In a universe as vast as ours, there are many forces, dimensions, and beings that we neither recognize nor understand. To deny these possibilities reflects a life without wonder. There will always be those who fear anything outside of their closed life, and unfortunately, what one fears, one will often deny and try to destroy.

CHAPTER 2

There was a time when the distances between our world and those we consider imaginary were no further than a bend in the road. Each cavern and hollow tree was a doorway to another world. Humans recognized life in all things. The streams sang and the winds whispered ancient words into the ears of whoever would listen. Every blade of grass and flower had a story to tell. In the blink of an eye, one could explore worlds and seek out knowledge that enlightened life. Shadows were not just shadows and woods were not just trees and clouds were not just pretty. There was life and purpose in all things and there was loving interaction between the worlds.[1]

Of all the creatures of the Faerie Realm, unicorns are the most hesitant to reveal themselves. They are elusive and spend most of their time by themselves. Although often believed to exist only in the most inaccessible environments, they do live in special places in nature which always remain a little wild. They have been seen in forests, mountains, deserts, and by the seas. Though hard to spot in all of these environments, their pathways and habitats become more recognizable with just a little knowledge and perception. The more you know about the unicorn, both myth and fact, the easier it will be to invite its essence and energy into your life.

Many have been touched by the unicorn's magic without ever truly realizing it. For some, there have been real life encounters, encounters that heralded transformations. Many others have had a life-long fascination with unicorns through story, art, and even dreams, an interest no less significant than a real life encounter! Unfortunately, few know how to decipher and enhance this relationship. Few know how to progress to the next step.

Even if considered only a symbol, the unicorn generates tremendous power and energy, the image embodying great magic, mysticism, and wonder. On one level, the unicorn serves as an archetype, "a matrix or a key image which gives shape and direction to energies arising out of the primal source of all being."[2]

---

[1] Ted Andrews, *Enchantment of the Faerie Realm* (St. Paul: Llewellyn Publications, 1993), p. 3.
[2] R.J. Stewart, *The Underworld Initiation* (Northamptonshire: Aquarian Press, 1985), p. 92.

Archetypes are universal, reflecting a primal energy pattern. Just as the moon reflects the light of the sun, symbols and images reflect an archetypal energy at play within our lives. When we work with archetypes, we are lead back to our own primal source. The journey becomes part of the sacred quest.

Carl Jung spoke of archetypes as part of the "collective unconscious," something we all share. The fact that images and tales of the unicorn are found within most major cultures of the world lends even more validity to the unicorn being an archetypal image. All archetypal images are magickal when we use them as symbols of spiritual significance. The greater the significance we attach to the image, the greater the power and the magick it will hold.

Embracing the Unicorn's Energy

Whether experienced as a symbol or as a living creature, the unicorn's energy must still be embraced for its fullest benefit. Any encounter with a unicorn will release its energy and essence into our lives. For the fullest benefit, though, we must take an active role in the interplay with that energy.

Become Conscious of the Unicorn in Your Life

Remember that the unicorn is more than a fanciful or mythical creature: it has many levels of significance. Begin by taking some time to reflect upon the unicorn's image, its most obvious significance. What does the unicorn represent for you personally?

Encounters take many forms and their effects are varied. These encounters may occur through dreams, photographs, or paintings. They may occur through stuffed toys or figurines which catch your eye. They may occur through being drawn to a book such as this one. Every time a unicorn catches your attention, there is an encounter affecting some aspect of your life. Often the effects are atavistic—uncontrolled and unrecognized for what they truly are.

Try to relate the encounter directly to your life and its events. What does it mean to you? How do you normally experience the unicorn? Through art? Dreams? In real life? When have you been most drawn to the unicorn? What was going on in your life at that time, especially prior to and just after the encounter? What were some of the major events in your life at that time? Are there times of the year when your encounters are more frequent? Less frequent? Are there times in your life when encounters have been most frequent? Absent? Are there particular goals or projects that you have been more focused upon around the time of the encounters?

Use the Unicorn Journal described in Chapter 1 to keep track of your encounters, help you to identify patterns, and where the unicorn energy manifests itself in your life. The Unicorn Journal helps effectively focus the energy for your benefit.

ALIGN YOURSELF DEEPLY WITH THE UNICORN

Study what different societies and traditions have taught about the unicorn. This book and those listed in the bibliography will help in this task. Pay particular attention to stories, myths, and correspondences that stand out for you. Note the origin of those stories and what these societies teach about the unicorn. This adds depth to your own associations.

Adding depth to your unicorn associations is a magickal process, part of the spiritual journey. The meditations, visualizations, and physical activities help integrate new dimensions of the unicorn energy into your own. By adopting, adapting, and absorbing other teachings to your own personal bank, you intensify your own unicorn energy.

Take time to contemplate and assimilate the new teachings on a regular basis. The amount of time set aside for this isn't important. Do this regularly and in conjunction with your other work. How do the new teachings reflect and add to your understanding of past encounters and their effects within your life? Each time you contemplate your encounters, you will find more golden threads tying the unicorn to events within your life.

You will also want to contemplate your unicorn encounters after performing the exercises in this book. What was your inner reaction to the experience of the exercise? What effects did the exercise have on the events of your day-to-day life. These activities will help you recognize the connection and impact of the unicorn on your life.

GROUND YOUR EXPERIENCE WITH THE UNICORN

Contact with more subtle realms of life can have a tendency to draw our attention away from the focus of our daily physical life. This contact should enhance our physical life, not distract from it. It is important to stay grounded and centered, especially when working with the strong energies of the Faerie Realm. Because the Faerie Realm intersects our own world, the energies of its creatures are often strongly experienced, but not always recognized.

The post-exercise process—contemplation on the inner reaction and outer assessment—will initiate the grounding, but something more physical is needed as well. Record your impressions and feelings in the Unicorn Journal. Writing about your feelings in a journal serves as a trigger to the subconscious. As events in your life unfold in the following few days, you will be able to recognize the influence of the unicorn and its energy within your life.

> *O Unicorn among the cedars,*
> *To whom no magic charm can lead us,*
> *White childhood moving like a sigh*
> *Through the green woods unharmed in thy*
> *Sophisticated innocence,*
> *To call thy true love to the dance...*
>
> W.H. Auden
> "New Year Letters"
> *Collected Short Poems*

The information and the exercises in this book are designed to take you into deeper expressions of the unicorn's archetypal energy within your life. The greater and stronger the focus, the greater and stronger the play of energy. The exercises will align you with the spiritual energies of the unicorn and open the doors to its earthly habitats, helping you seek out and invite a more tangible encounter.

When working with the unicorn energy, use the unicorn stance in Chapter 3, Exercise 3, before and after each exercise. This honors the unicorn, bringing your essence and energy into resonance with it, and helps eliminate the "spacy" feelings that can result from meditations.

Like the white hart of the Celtic tradition which leads hunters into the woods and into adventures that change their lives forever, the unicorn invites change into our lives. When we venture into the world of the unicorn, we are venturing into the world of sacred possibilities. As we open ourselves to that experience, we will never be the same. The unicorn encounter will be both haunting and inspiring to the soul.

The unicorn comes nobly and gently to those with an open heart. Its sweet breath will comfort those who are lost and alone. Its horn will heal all wounds—whether real or imagined. And it will dance for those who will embrace their dreams!

The Secret World of the Unicorn

Unicorns are born in complete seclusion. Though born with blue eyes, they begin to darken after ten to twelve months and have changed completely after the magickal time of a year and a day. One ancient European belief is that the eyes become blue again after 1000 years. How long a unicorn lives is still unknown.

From the moment they are born, their senses are much more acute than those of any other animal. Unicorns can detect the softest whisper of a breeze before it enters its territory, the subtlest of movement, the fragrance of a flower a mile away. Unicorns are so fast they seem to fly and disappear magically. Because their senses are so highly developed, they rarely allow themselves to be seen. Casual human contact is virtually nonexistent.

UNICORN GIFTS

Many gifts, blessings, and wonders are shared, many secrets and sacred confidences entrusted to those who open their hearts to the unicorn quest.

- understanding the language of animals
- renewed innocence and wonder
- ability to recognize deception
- healing in many forms
- knowledge of the mysteries of plants, herbs and trees
- heightened sexuality— physical and spiritual
- increased productivity in personal endeavors
- new levels of love and devotion
- intimate contact with beings of the Faerie Realm
- understanding of physical and spiritual alchemy
- ability to read signs and omens in nature
- heightened sensitivity
- strengthened clairvoyance.
- sense of nobility as an individual
- increased serenity in daily life
- increased spiritual illumination
- discovery of the reality of dreams
- increased awareness of the sacred within life
- mystery of astral flight and levitation
- renewed joy and hope

CHAPTER 2

Although there are tales about only one unicorn upon the earth at a time, this has never been generally accepted, and is definitely untrue. This belief seems to be a carryover from the phoenix myth, in which only one phoenix is alive on the planet at any one time. The phoenix lives to be 500 years old and then dies amidst flames; out of its ashes rises the next phoenix. Since there is a strong relationship between the phoenix and the unicorn, it is not unusual to have similar tales arise.

Unicorns are born without fear and with a great love for play. Running and jumping are joys to them, which is why they are often seen with deer. They have a great love of flowers, both the scent and the look. The young love wild blackberries and raspberries. They understand the language of all animals, but have a special relationship with birds. They protect the animals of their environments and often help feed the other animals, going so far as to use their horns to dig holes for squirrels or knock fruit and nuts from trees. They have been known to free animals from traps.

There is a great gentleness and lack of guile, a quality which lead to it's becoming a symbol for early Christianity. This same lack of guile was associated with one of the apostles—Bartholomew (Nathaniel)—the one in whom Jesus found no guile.

Unicorns are born with the single horn or *alicorn*, probably their most outstanding and most magical characteristic. The alicorn was prized by popes and kings and sought by nobility and common folk alike. The alicorn provides protection against evil and has the ability to detect poisons and counteract them. During the 14th century, poisoning was a common way to deal with one's enemies. The alicorn was set in the middle of a table. If a dew formed upon it, the food was poisoned.

Unicorns are found in diverse environments. Although solitary, they will occasionally gather in small groups of two, three, or four at a favorite and protected water source, often near a waterfall, to drink and share each other's company.

In the autumn, the season of rut, even greater gentleness is demonstrated by the male with the female. When the mating is over, the male stays around to guard and watch from a distance, leaving the female to

TREASURES OF THE UNICORN

birth and rear the young unicorn. Like humans, the unicorn is born approximately nine months after conception. The male, although distant, watches over the two and their safety, until the young is strong and able to live on its own.

Although usually depicted as white, many tales tell of colored unicorns as well. Whatever the overall color, the hooves are usually depicted as silver, and the alicorn most often with a pearl iridescence. This iridescence seems to change with the light, comparable to the iridescence of the dragon fly.

Some dragonflies have color pigments in their skin, but their colors are generally caused in the same manner as rainbows:

> Structures in their shell scatter and refract the light, making them look iridescent green and blue. As they age, they may pass through several color changes.... The dragonfly and damselfly reflect and work with the sun and light. The light changes throughout the day. The dragonfly and damselfly undergo their own transformations.[3]

The alicorn is believed to refract light and so its iridescence shifts throughout the day with the changing light.

Many societies consider the dragonfly a distant relative to the dragons of lore. Dragons are also part of the Faerie Realm, just as is the phoenix, the unicorn, and other fantastic creatures. Like the unicorn and the phoenix, the unicorn and the dragon also have a unique relationship.

Unicorns can move silently through any environment, including the most densely forested areas, its presence often heralded by a soft tinkling sound of tiny silver bells, as if carried upon a breeze—but only when the unicorn wishes. The Chinese liken this sound to a thousand soft chimes. While the voice of the unicorn is sweet and delicate, it abhors fighting, but on those rare occasions, it demonstrates a fierceness that is almost unsurpassed.

---

[3] Ted Andrews, *Animal-Speak* (St. Paul: Llewellyn Publications, 1993), pp. 341-342.

CHAPTER 2

The qualities of the unicorn are diverse. Throughout the book, we will examine some of the predominant ones. The significance of the unicorn plays a unique role in each life, with its own individual "twist." Remember that images and symbols touch both our objective and subjective realities, with an exoteric and an esoteric aspect. The unicorn is no exception. The unicorn, however, is also a living creature, making its force more definable in some ways and also more powerful than a mere symbol.

Many qualities and characteristics are associated with the unicorn. Some of the more important traits are gentleness and purity, sexuality and fertility, and healing and transformation. These are discussed below, but additional important traits (but by no means all) include ferocity, power, immortality, serenity, nobility, alchemy, innocence, sacredness, chastity, good fortune, new life, intuition, religiousness, sacrifice, gracefulness, love, solitude, strength, wisdom, trust, sensitivity, solitude, protection, and dreams.

GENTLENESS AND PURITY

The unicorn is so gentle and soft hearted it walks upon the grass without crushing it, bending the blades rather than breaking them, and prizes this quality in humans. The unicorn will bow to gentleness and purity among mortals and its glance will overpower all emotion except gentle love. These are the unicorn's qualities that restore lost innocence. Nobility of spirit begins with gentleness and purity and this is what the unicorn awakens and teaches. These qualities are innate and of the heart, not of the body. Unfortunately, few people know how to express gentleness and purity within their lives. The unicorn reminds us how to do this.

SEXUALITY AND FERTILITY

The unicorn holds the key to the mysteries of sexuality, both physical and spiritual, awakening new surges of the creative life force. While the unicorn is typically considered an archetypal female symbol, the single horn has often been viewed as a phallic symbol. As a symbol of the male and female coming together, uniting on any level, new birth occurs. When these elements unite within us, we give birth to the Holy Child that is our true essence. The unicorn holds the knowledge of the *mystic marriage*, the alchemical blending of the male and female both physically and spiritually, awakening new levels and expressions of sexuality and renewing our fertility in all areas of our life.

Healing and Transformation

Everything about the unicorn is tied to healing, and the transformations that healing brings. True healing is multidimensional, touching us physically, emotionally, mentally, and spiritually. Healing requires a change in consciousness. The unicorn touches the part of us we have long forgotten, reminding us that prayers are supposed to be answered. Miracles are supposed to happen; healing is supposed to occur. As children, everything was possible. The unicorn teaches us that if we change our imaginings, we change our world.

In Search of the Unicorn

Although the unicorn has been found in most natural environments, ranging from the deserts to the forests and from the seas to the mountains, the forested environment is where encounters are most likely to occur. These are the places where the signs of the unicorn's presence are more easily determined. The forested environments where unicorns live have certain characteristics in common. There will be particular trees, wild flowers, animals, insects, and other natural elements the unicorn likes.

Unicorns love secluded areas. The forest must have an untamed area, one rarely frequented by humans. Unicorns are often seen near water and love waterfalls. They will sometimes intermingle with herds of horses or deer and frequent meadows of wild flowers and butterflies. Their hoof prints, almost heart shaped in appearance, are more visible in the early morning dew and in the first early morning frost of the autumn. Sleeping spots can be matted ferns and soft green moss.

The more there are of these elements unicorns prefer, the higher the probability the unicorn will be seen. The following paragraphs describe the particular kinds of trees, flowers and plants, and animals most often associated with unicorns.

TREES

The unicorn prefers apple, sugar maple, holly, and cedar trees as well as lilacs. The tree most sacred to the unicorn is the apple. A common legend tells of how the unicorn hides its treasures in a cedar box beneath the apple tree, and the unicorn often makes it home there and sometimes can be seen near an apple tree on moonlit nights.

The Faerie Realm has a long association with the apple tree. Apple blossoms draw out great numbers of fairies who help promote feelings of happiness. The spirit of the apple tree works with the unicorn, and in the spring will often appear with the unicorn in the form of a beautifully enticing woman. Together, they open the heart to new realms of love.

The cedar tree, with a protective and healing spirit, is also special to the unicorn. Boxes of cedar house some of the most sacred and valuable treasures of the unicorn. We see remnants of this in today's world where cedar boxes with paintings of unicorns can be seen in many gift stores. The spirit of the cedar tree helps stimulate dreams of the unicorn.

Unicorns have a great love for wild honey and maple syrup. Wild bee hives and sugar maple trees are places likely to be visited or even inhabited by the unicorn. Meditating on the unicorn near a maple tree dynamically accesses the creative energies of the unicorn and can help invite the unicorn's assistance in fulfilling dreams.

The lilac is a also a favorite of the unicorn, especially in the spring. The fragrance draws the unicorn and it likes to wear garlands of flowers, especially pink and purple ones. Meadows with lilac bushes are wonderful places to meditate on the unicorn and extend it an invitation to become a part of your life.

The holly is also important to the unicorn. The holly spirit often guards many spirits and fairy beings, sharing this role with the unicorn. Meditating on the unicorn near holly is a powerful way of tapping into the unicorn's healing energies.

In Celtic lunar astrology, the holly tree is associated with the period of July 8th through August 4th, representing the evergreen aspect of the soul, the earth goddess, and the transformational aspect and powers of the goddess. It is a time of the festival of Lammas, or the beginning of autumn in the seasonal calendar. Autumn is also the mating season of the unicorn and in the Celtic tradition, this month was also associated with the unicorn and its transformational powers. August is an ideal month to establish or strengthen connection to the unicorn.

FLOWERS AND PLANTS

Unicorns have a great love for flowers, particularly wild flowers. They will often seek out flowered meadows for frolicking and sleeping. Birds will often gather the flowers and garland the unicorn's horn, mane, and tail as it sleeps. Flowers and plants associated with the unicorn are clover, lilac, apple blossoms, unicorn plant, centaury, chicory, ferns, and mosses.

Clover is one of the unicorn's favorites, and it particularly likes to lie in fields of red clover. The fairies of clover reveal themselves readily to those who display kindness, so there is great compatibility and fondness between the unicorn and clover. During the full moon, the unicorn is drawn more to meadows with white clover and the meadows with purple and red at other times. Washing the eyes with clover water can promote seeing and feeling the presence of the unicorn.

In the spring when the lavender lilac blossoms fill the air with their fragrance, the unicorn is usually not far away. Around lilacs in bloom, individuals are likely to hear the silver bells that herald the presence of the unicorns.

One of the more important flowers for those of us in North America is the unicorn root, also known as *aletris farinosa* of the lily family (*liliaceae*). The flower stems are tubular, about one to three feet high, and topped with tiny bell-shaped flowers; thus, its name "the unicorn root." This is an excellent plant to meditate with and open the doors to unicorn encounters. It is found in eastern and central U.S. at the edges of swampy or wet woods[4] and can indicate of a unicorn lives in that environment.

The unicorn enjoys ferns and soft green moss for making bedding. Matted but unbroken ferns can indicate the unicorn has slept nearby. Chicory and the nature spirits associated with it help stimulate selfless love and a greater sense of motherliness—qualities similar to the unicorn's. Centaury nature spirits stimulate a stronger sense of self-realization. Since the unicorn helps us to remember our lost dreams can be found and, these nature spirits help us in realizing and following our own life quest.

> **Unicorn Root**
> *Also known as colic root, star grass, and true unicorn root, this plant is part of the lily family. When found at the edges of woods and fields, it can indicate the presence or home of the unicorn.*

ANIMALS

Unicorns are the protectors of all animal life, often intermingling with herds of deer and horses. This is most common at dawn and dusk, or when human activity is more prominent. Animals associated with the unicorn include the peacock, butterflies, nightingale, hummingbirds, woodpeckers, nuthatches, doves, and deer and horses.

---

[4] LeArta A. Moulton, *Herb Walk* (Provo: Gluten Co., Inc., 1979), pp. 88-89.

Unicorns have a special relationship with all birds. Birds have been known to decorate their horns, manes, and tails while they rest in fields of

Unicorns will often inermingle with deer. Much of medieval art depicted the two together in a wood. Such depictions were often symbolic of the three-fold nature of humans. The forest represented the "body," the deer represented "the soul," and the unicorn represented "the spirit." They were often coupled in art for they both could lead the true master in and out of life— in and out of the body.

flowers. Perching upon the alicorn seems to be a popular activity for birds, particularly the dove. Birds with traditionally gentle and magickal associations seem to be most strongly connected to unicorns.[5]

---

[5] The myths and lore of these birds are discussed in greater detail in *Animal Speak* by Ted Andrews (St. Paul: Llewellyn Publications, 1993).

CHAPTER 2

The peacock is one of the closest companions to the unicorn. This bird itself has been vested with much lore throughout the ages. Powerful and protective, it warns the unicorn of danger or intruders.

The peacock was considered sacred in Egypt because it destroyed poisonous snakes and was regarded as second only to the Ibis. The peacock also has links to the ancient phoenix. Thus, like the unicorn, the peacock is an animal of healing and purification, so it is natural that the unicorn and the peacock should have such a strong relationship. Meditating with peacock feathers can open up visions of the unicorn.

Butterflies also have a strong connection to the unicorn. The butterfly, like the unicorn, has been a symbol of transformation and joy. Many traditions speak of fairies and nature spirits traveling on the backs of butterflies, and the unicorn is drawn to fields where butterflies are abundant. Butterflies can usually be seen adorning the unicorn and they, like the unicorn, teach us that change is good and that it is important to take advantage of these kind of opportunities.

Change is what makes life a dance of joy.

A Family of Unicorns

EXERCISE 2: Preparing for the Unicorn Quest

BENEFITS
- heightens life reverence
- awakens inner child
- leads to real life encounters

There are many things we can do to help in our quest of the unicorn—be it for a real life encounter or to open ourselves spiritually to the transforming powers.

Begin by learning as much as possible about unicorns. Meditate and reflect upon them. Find artwork or drawings of unicorns, keep them around you, and meditate and reflects upon them. Draw your own unicorns.

Spend time in nature! Become more cognizant of the beauties and wonders of nature and take time regularly to appreciate them. Become more aware of the abuses of nature and do your part to clean them up, demonstrating reverence for nature.

Be generous and loving in your dealings with others. Perform, as it has become popularly termed, "random acts of kindness." Perform them anonymously. One way I do this is to periodically pick a name from the phone book and send a gift to the individual. Sometimes it is a flower arrangement, sometimes a crystal, and sometimes just a dollar. I usually place a note inside that simply says: "Just because...."

And always keep the child within you alive. Find joy in the little things: the beauty of a flower, the song that stays with you all day, a creative or artistic activity. Work on developing the qualities honored and respected by the unicorn:

Be free in your thinking and creativity!
(Break free of the limitations and structures of society.)

Be open to new ideas and possibilities!
(Break free of the perceptions of the past and present.)

Be responsible and generous!
(Attend to obligations and opportunities for kindness.)

Be true to your heart!
(Attend to hopes, wishes, and dreams, for we are never given them without also being given opportunities to make them reality.)

THE BEST PLACES TO ENCOUNTER UNICORNS

flower meadows hidden from the general public

woods and forests

near waterfalls

where nature stills remains wild

near apple and cedar trees
(especially on moonlit nights)

where holly grows wild and free
(especially between July 8 and August 4)

at gathering spots for butterflies

near streams abundant with dragonflies

where strawberries grow wild

where swans are found

THE BEST TIMES
TO ENCOUNTER UNICORNS

dawn and dusk
(traditional 'tween times)

solstices and equinoxes

autumn equinox and throughout the
autumn season

moonlit nights
(especially near apple trees and orchards)

while the morning dew is still
upon the ground

when frost covers the ground,
(particularly the first frost)

From July 8 - August 4
(the Celtic month of Tinne)

at the time of the Fire Festival of Lammas

while the Morning Star is shining
in the pre-dawn sky

sunset and sunrise

ENCOUNTER GUIDELINES

If your quest for the unicorn is to encompass a real life encounter, there are guidelines you should always follow:

1. Enter the woods reverently and with a sense of awe—as if you are the first person to ever set foot within them.

2. Wear no clothing or articles from dead animals.

3. Wear no perfumes, deodorants or scents.

   You may use mint leaves as a fragrance, but only if they are picked with permission and respect and in the woods you are seeking.

4. Take no food of any dead animals with you.

   Fruits are OK, especially apples.

5. Walk normally, but slowly and quietly.

   Attempts to sneak will be perceived.

6. Avoid camouflage clothing. Dress normally.

7. If staying over night, build no fire and avoid hunting or fishing.

8. If accompanied by another, talk little and only in whispered tones.

9. Take no pets.

10. Watch carefully, as unicorns are often first seen out of the corners of the eyes, and they often appear and disappear in the blink of an eye.

SOME ENCOUNTER CAUTIONS

If you are fortunate in your seeking, remember:

DO NOT TRY TO FEED, TOUCH, OR CAPTURE!

> This more than anything
> Will offend the unicorn.
> And a hope will be lost
> That may never again be born.

When we open to the unicorn, our lives will be permeated by the awesome power of nature. But the unicorn is part of the realm of enchantment as well. When we embrace one, we also embrace the other. They are inseparable.

We will learn to embrace ourselves as a conscious living force. We will learn to feel every touch as a passing of power to hurt or to heal. We will hear every thought and word as a force to curse or bless. We will experience every step of our life as a prayer of hope and transformation.

> For he comes, the human child,
> To the waters and the wild
> With a faery, hand in hand,
> From a world more full of weeping than he can understand.[6]

---

[6] W.B. Yeats. "The Stolen Child," in *Collected Poems of W.B. Yeats*, ed. Richard J. Finneran (New York: MacMillan Publishing Company, 1989), p. 19.

CHAPTER 3

The Alicorn's Magic

When God created the earth, he made a
river which flowed from the Garden of
Eden....Then God told Adam to name the
animals...and the first animal he named
was the unicorn. When the Lord heard the
name that Adam had spoken, he reached
down and touched the tip of the single horn
growing from the animal's forehead. From
that moment on, the unicorn was elevated
above other beasts.

Nancy Hathaway
*The Unicorn**
pp. 29-30

* Nancy Hathaway, *The Unicorn* (New York: Viking Press, 1980), pp. 29-30. From The *Unicorn* by Nancy Hathaway. Copyright ©1980 by Nancy Hathaway and Rosebud Books, Inc. Used by permission of Viking Penguin, a division of Penguin Books USA, Inc.

The unicorn's most mystical aspect, the alicorn (from the Latin *alicorne*), has been described and depicted in a variety of ways. To some, the horn has a mother of pearl iridescence. To others, it is rainbow hued or multicolored. It has even been described as tricolored (red, white, and black). Although the descriptions of the alicorne's color has varied, it is most often described as a spiral with a luminous appearance.

The alicorn was highly prized for its healing capabilities. When it is near anything poisonous, it will sweat, exuding a honey-like substance that will counteract all toxins. Even as far back as the 4th century BC, there was a strong belief that the alicorn could neutralize poisons. The Greek physician Ctesius wrote that water or wine left standing for several hours in a beaker made of the alicorn would be cleansed of poisons and infections of all kinds.[1]

Many believed the superstition of "water conning," that snakes and serpents loosed their venom into the water of rivers at night so other animals could not drink. The unicorn, by dipping its horn into the river, would purify the waters so animals could then drink freely. This belief arose during a critical point in European history. At this time typhoid was rampant, and many believed that it was carried through the water supply. In 1389, John of Hesse reported witnessing a water conning and subsequent unicorn purification during a visit to the Holy Land. His report generated a great interest in the alicorn.

During the Middle Ages and Renaissance in Europe, the general public's interest in the unicorn became fueled by the wondrous healing power of the alicorn. Unfortunately, this interest was often at the expense of the unicorn and any similar animal. The 12th century mystic Hildegarde de Bingen, who has grown popular in our recent times, promoted the killing of the unicorn for its many benefits:

- shoes of unicorn hide kept feet healthy,
- belts of unicorn leather prevented fevers and plague,

---

[1] Nancy Hathaway, *The Unicorn* (New York: Viking Press, 1980), p. 114.

- unicorn liver, ground and mashed with egg yolks, cured leprosy, and

- the horn saved lives (that is, if God didn't want the patient to die).

During this period of history, many of the horns that passed for alicorns were either rhinoceros or narwhal. King Edward I of England possessed these horns, as did Charles VI. Pope Clement (1553) gave a horn to Henry II of France. Phillip II of Spain owned twelve. Mary, Queen of Scots, possessed one as well, and the list goes on.[2]

narwal

This led to great superstitious and ignorant slaughter of rhinos and narwhals. The rationale for such slaughter was superstitious and ignorant: *These animals were exotic and had single horns, so therefore they must be related to the unicorn!* Deception was often easy, especially during medieval times, and almost any exotic or unusual horn could be passed off as an alicorn.

rhinoceros

With the amount of fraud involved with supposed alicorns, tests to distinguish the true alicorn from the false were devised. The four most common tests reflected the following beliefs:

- A true alicorn, when placed in water, would cause the water to bubble as if boiling, yet the water remained cold.

- A true alicorn, when laid on top of a piece of silk resting on a burning coal, would keep the silk from burning.

---

[2] Nancy Hathaway, *The Unicorn* (New York: Viking Press, 1980), p. 144.

- A true alicorn placed near a poisonous plant, animal, or substance would cause the poison source to burst and die.
- A true alicorn, placed in a ring drawn upon the floor prevented a spider from crossing the line to leave the circle. The spider would then starve to death.[3]

In truth, the power of the alicorn is probably as much symbolic as real, but it still has the ability to stir the human spirit. To many, imagination and believing are the only forms of magic left in the world. If true, then imagination and believing, when used properly, are then the most powerful forms of magic. We must remember, however, the imaginative world and the unreal world are not the same.

The image-creating faculty of the mind is called imagination. Through this ability we open ourselves to the spiritual background of physical life. We begin to see the spiritual essences and energies surrounding and interplaying with the physical world.

Most people consider imagination some form of level beyond the normal sensory world. Through creative imagination, we awaken a new awareness, a new kind of experience in color and form to our real world. Imagination triggers higher forms of inspiration and intuition. Imagination helps us to understand the spiritual hierarchies that inhabit our lives, revealing the beings and forces that inhabit the supersensible world around us.

The unicorn and its wondrous horn never fail to create a sense of enchantment. The image alone stirs the imagination and nudges our lost sense of belief. In this book, you will learn how to use this image to bless your live with wondrous change.

---

[3] Bruce Coville, *The Unicorn Treasury* (New York: Doubleday, 1988), p. 3.

Hidden Significance of the Alicorn

The most symbolic aspect of the unicorn, the alicorn—its shape, size, color, and every other aspect—is filled with hidden significance. The more we know of these aspects, the greater will be the energy play within our lives as we work with the alicorn.

Symbols touch both objective and subjective realities. Tools to open various doors to realms existing beyond our rational environment, symbols span the worlds of thought and feeling. They provide a means of communicating with the world of hidden realities, expressing what we have no words for. By working with symbols, we open doorways to our more intuitive self. Through the image of the unicorn, we tap into the energies it represents.

Symbols change as we grow and change. The greater significance we find within a symbol, the more power that symbol will have within our life. Strong symbols, symbols that we align with on multiple levels, evolve and expand our awareness, becoming a source of knowledge and higher initiation.

Archetypal symbols express themselves in myriad ways, adapting to the individual. With the archetypal aspects of the unicorn, its energy is likely to be discernible. Each person will experience its energy in a unique way. The unicorn, more than a reflection of archetypal force, has a life of its own.

Choosing to seek the unicorn invites its archetypal force into your life. Knowledge of the unicorn will unfold as you nurture the symbol; as your awareness of the unicorn grows (symbolic and real), the more its hidden essence and power will unfold and manifest within your life. This knowledge releases the unicorn's archetypal force.

The unicorn's alicorn has three main areas of symbolism:

- shape,
- spirals, and
- luminosity.

SHAPE

Many animals have horns or antlers, but few have singular horns such as the narwal and rhino. Of these few animals with singular horns, only the unicorn's emerges from the middle of the forehead. Antlers and horns have often been symbolic of higher consciousness and mental ability, like antennae, linking to higher forms of attunement. Encounters with horned and antlered animals often signal the need to pay attention to inner thoughts and perceptions. Antlers and horns typically grow behind the eyes and on the crown of the head, reflecting heightened perception.

In the unicorn, the horn grows from the middle of the forehead, above and between the eyes. This relates to the brow chakra or third eye area of traditional metaphysics. The center for intuition, creative imagination, and heightened perception, the center for inner vision and spiritual insight resides in this area in humans.

The appearance of the unicorn brings heightened perceptions, increasing the strength and accuracy of intuition. Auric vision may awaken, as may spirit vision (particularly vision of nature spirits, fairies, and elves). Those with a life long interest in the unicorn have probably had many Faerie Realm encounters, but failed to recognize them for what they were. For clarification of Faerie Realm encounters, see my *Enchantment of the Faerie Realm.*

Besides the placement of the alicorn, the shape of it has phallic significance. Sexual energies are physical manifestations of more dynamic spiritual energies at play. An animal of great purity and spirituality, the unicorn was often depicted in sensual scapes with erotic connotations. Frequently depicted with virginal or alluring, voluptuous women, sometimes naked, the unicorn represented the lover, trapped and seduced by its beloved.

While it may seem contradictory that the innocent unicorn is linked with the sensual and seductive female, sensuality and sexuality are frequently misunderstood, particularly their mystical aspects. The unicorn teaches that the human process of alchemy is related directly to true sexual energies.

When adults begin to explore and align with the unicorn, there will be a stronger stimulation of sexual energy, not only in ourselves, but also in those around us. Others begin to respond more strongly, lovingly, and sensually to us. A soft, subtle effect, but stimulating of sensuality. In many ways, the alicorn awakens a rebirth of these energies, as if coming to new life or exposed to fresh air. For children, the alicorn awakens the creative imagination and stimulates encounters with the Faerie Realm. Children themselves seem to take on a more luminous aspect.

Initially, the healing aspect may draw children. At a recent conference, I was approached by a social worker who had spent great amounts of time in homes serving as a court representative for abused children. She mentioned finding paintings and figurines of unicorns in many of the homes. In a number of these homes, the children had been sexually abused. I believe the children's fascination with the unicorn may be linked to their trying to heal themselves. Abuse robs children of their innocence, childhood, and purity. A violent act, abuse kills the child on some level.

The primary function of sexuality is conception and new birth. Maybe on a subconscious level, we are drawn instinctively to the unicorn to heal where wounds are deepest. Maybe the unicorn, even with its phallic aspects, restores a child's sense of innocence and purity. Since the unicorn is the most gentle, loving, and healing of all creatures, maybe its essence is required to restore such a loss of innocence and to stimulate a new birth. Maybe the unicorn initiates rebirth in spite of the death that occurred through the abuse.

The alicorn is the magic wand, one half of the creative principle of life. It is the initiator, the stimulus, the catalyst. It magnifies and directs the creative process. Used in many societies around the world, the prop wand of the stage magician is probably familiar to many. A true wand serves a creative function in the process of transformation. Wands are channels for energy.

The unicorn possesses combined female and male aspects, symbolizing birth and initiation. The horse has often been tied to the archetypal female energies. Nature and all within it is generally considered to be feminine. The unicorn is a feminine symbol with a prominent masculine aspect joined to it. The brow center, from which the alicorn rises, is the seat of the feminine energy within the human body. It is the center of our intuition and creative imagination. The alicorn in the forehead reflects the union of the male and the female.

In the unicorn, this combination of female and male aspects represents and activates a renewal of life so that the Holy Child within can be born. Anytime the two unite on any level, there is a creation of new energy. Our focus upon, search for, and alignment with the unicorn is an act of creating wholeness. Work with the unicorn renews our sacredness. It helps us find that place where there is no separation. It creates an intersection within our lives where all possibilities exist and are born.

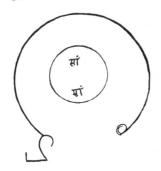

This yantra is a variation of one believed to cure disease when used ritually for 45 days.

Spirals

The spiral is one of the most common geometric forms found within nature, a symbol for expressing the ebb and flow of nature and life. The alicorn's spiral reflects change and transformation, the moving in and moving out. Circle and spiral dances were common in all societies, performed in imitation of the stars within the heavens. The spiral is manifestation. It is the path of evolution and involution.

In the Eastern tradition, there is a concept called *yantra*: "The Sanskrit word 'yantra' derives from the root 'yam' meaning to sustain, hold or support energy inherent in a particular element, object or concept."[4] The

---

[4] Madhu Khanna, *Yantra* (London: Thames & Hudson, 1979), p. 11.

yantra, then, is a geometric form that contains and activates a power or force. Many of these occult forms were used for communication with supernatural forces working between the heavens and the earth for a variety of functions, including healing.

The spiral is also sexual—physical and spiritual. It is a reflection of the primal creative life force within us, as in the DNA spiral. The spiral represents the movement of the *kundalini*, the sacred life force, symbolizing the conscious activation of the primal life force within us. Kundalini is the serpent power connecting all of our body's energy centers. Activating this force unfolds and manifests our highest potentials.

The kundalini is often misunderstood. Our primal, creative life force, the kundalini is already active or we would be dead. However, it can be stimulated into greater activity throughout the body, increasing sexual feelings, healing, and creativity in many fashions.

When the unicorn stimulates kundalini, the increased force is gentle. Often I hear individuals speaking of how painful kundalini exercises can be. This always triggers several warning bells. First, this falsely implies the kundalini was not active at all. We couldn't exist without kundalini activity. Second, this supports the myth that kundalini experiences are painful, at least initially, as if the pain reflects a necessary pushing energy through blocks within the body. This promotes the idea that suffering is necessary to spiritual growth.

I firmly believe the only good in suffering is learning how not to suffer. We do not have to traumatize ourselves to grow and evolve. Painful experiences indicate the exercises were inappropriate for the individual, comparable to running 300 volts through a 110 volt socket. The unicorn, on the other hand, can be a wonderful tool for gently stimulating the kundalini.

There has long been a belief that a kundalini experience can only be stimulated by a guru or highly evolved individual, but this is not necessarily true:

It is true that Kundalini may be triggered by someone who is adept *Shaktipat* (Kundalini awakening) by their mere presence. Not everyone in the presence of such a guru receives Shaktipat, however, and still others experience this energy quite spontaneously, without harm, and without gurus.[5]

Kundalini can be stimulated by an outside source, be it a person or an archetypal energy with which we have aligned ourselves. Kundalini is an activation of energy within us. Sometimes this is spontaneous; at other times, this has a definable trigger. That trigger can be meditation, rhythmic breathing, creative visualization, healing activity, artistic expression, contact with an individual of high energy, or any number of things. While it is not the purpose of this book to teach kundalini, it should be noted that those who align with the unicorn often undergo an increased activation of the kundalini.

This activation always elicits certain physiological and metaphysical effects. The most obvious is the stimulation of sexuality, with all of its biochemical and spiritual aspects. This activation can stimulate heightened perception and creative inspiration, and can make some individuals hypersensitive. This activation can also stimulate healing energies which can be self-directed or directed to others, can make dreams more colorful and lucid, and will create changes in consciousness. Much of this will be discussed later when we explore the alchemical aspects of the unicorn. For now, it is just important to realize that the unicorn is an archetypal image linked to our sexual life force.

LUMINOSITY

The alicorn has a luminous aspect which glows or shines. This luminosity (regardless of the color) ties the alicorn to the ancient image of the flaming sword. This is the sword of spiritual law within the physical world.

---

[5] Judith Anodea, *Wheels of Life* (St. Paul: Llewellyn Publications, 1988), pp. 37-38.

In ancient grail legends, the sword was also interchangeable with the spear which shed the blood of Jesus while upon the cross.

The sword, like the alicorn, is an ancient symbol of the divine force that animates all creation. It can be used to heal and bless, but its power lies in the willingness never to inflict wounds, even if it means receiving the wound ourselves. The law of the flaming sword was simple: "What one loses, one must find. What one hurts, one must heal. What one kills, one must restore to life."[6]

In esoteric Christianity, the flaming sword was associated with two of the great archangels, Michael and Auriel. Michael, considered the dragonslayer, is often depicted with a flaming sword. Michael, rather than slay the dragon, drove it into the depths of hell. The dragon, symbol of our primal, untransmuted elements, is not meant to be slain, but instead controlled and transmuted. The flaming sword was a tool for controlling and transmuting those elements so they work for rather than against us.

The unicorn awakens the dragon force and shows us how to gently control it within our life, helping us to purify the raw energy inherent within us. The dragon and unicorn are powerful companions. Together they blend strength and gentleness in a manner that cannot be matched, which is especially important in the initiatory process known as "Meeting the Dwellers on the Threshold." These roles will be explored more fully in the chapter on alchemy.

The flaming sword is also linked with the archangel Auriel. Auriel is the traditional governor of the summer season and considered the angel of beauty and vision, overseeing the nature realm, including all of those beings associated with it. Auriel is often considered the tallest of the archangels, with eyes that can see across eternity. Opening ourselves to Auriel can foster vision of all of those beings and creatures within the Faerie Realm, including the unicorn. Auriel guides our use of the unicorn force for personal transformation.

---

[6] Ted Andrews, *The Occult Christ: Angelic Mysteries & Divine Feminine* (St. Paul: Llewellyn Publications, 1993), pp. 131-134, 181-182.

Many colors have been attributed to the alicorn, and these can reveal much. Color is a concentration of light frequency and has the ability to affect us physically, emotionally, mentally, and spiritually. The alicorn's shine can tell us where the new birth and transformations are likely to occur.

Some colors are warm and some are depressing. Some colors uplift and some colors aggravate. A study of light and color can help understanding both the physiological and symbolic aspects of light and color.

For those who are interested in healing, the unicorn can be a valuable source, especially for individuals practicing color therapy. The luminosity of the alicorn, along with the color, can be used to stabilize physical, emotional, mental, and spiritual conditions. The unicorn and color therapy are most compatible!

CHAPTER 3

EXERCISE 3:   # Dance of the Unicorn

BENEFITS
- greater unicorn rapport
- healing
- gentle strength
- intuition

Dance and movement actualize energy. Even simple physical movements and postures can create changes in consciousness. Magickal dance is a way of using physical behavior to release and activate very real energies. Focused movement aligns the hemispheres of the brain, stimulating the intuitive faculty and creating electrical changes in the body and mind. These changes help us to transcend normal perceptions.

Different postures and movements will activate different energies and forces. Physical movement, combined with creative imagination, opens the ability to touch all worlds, placing a person at the gateway of all dimensions. The right movements, combined with the proper creative visualization, allow us to enter and exit through that gateway.

Imitation is one of the most common and powerful forms of magickal dance. Shamans imitate the movements of animals as a means of attuning themselves to the animals, to bring their energy into play more dynamically and personally. Imitative dancing is an important part of the shapeshifting process—the process of transforming your energy. Shapeshifting aligns energy, usually with an animal in nature, so a person can express that animal's qualities more effectively. In other words, if we need to be more bear-like in a situation, by posturing and moving like a bear, we can create the electrical changes in ourselves that are more resonant with the bear. Thus it becomes easier to express the qualities of that bear.

Many societies had movements and postures associated with animals, both real and mythic. These postures, when used in conjunction with other meditations, empower. We can apply this to our unicorn exploration as well.

In Northern Shaolin Long-Fist Sword techniques, there are eight fundamental stances. Two of these have great application for unicorn quests. These stances do not require an actual sword. A knife, athame, or a stick or your own creative imagination will more than suffice.

The traditional horse stance and the movement from the horse stance into the unicorn stance are two useful imitations. After learning these two, do not be afraid to adapt them. I use these two and several variations for certain magickal rituals and exercises that I perform in my personal spiritual work with the unicorn.

When I do workshops on magickal dance, I frequently teach the group simple dance rituals that elicit quick and definite effects. In this way, the group experiences and confirms for themselves how much more quickly results are achieved when the proper movement is used in conjunction with meditation or rituals. The group of magickal dances that I teach most frequently are connected to the fantastic creatures—the unicorn, the dragon, and the phoenix.

The unicorn stance is basic, but very powerful. Performing it every day aligns us with the unicorn energy, and thus it can be done as both a morning and evening ritual as well as in conjunction with other meditations and exercises. The unicorn stance used as a prelude to other meditative exercises found within this book will enhance the overall effectiveness of the exercises.

The unicorn stance can also be expanded into an entire dance ritual for groups involving costumes and all of the other elements of magickal dance. The various techniques and elements of spiritual and ceremonial dance can be found in my book, *Magickal Dance*.

The most important thing to remember is *do not be afraid to adapt!* Your relationship with the unicorn must be open and develop in its own way. Although unicorn quests have certain elements that are universal, each of us finds our own quest has unique differences from every other quest.

THE HORSE STANCE

(Ma Bu)

To assume the horse stance, begin with the feet parallel and placed slightly wider than shoulder width. Then move your feet further apart, widening the stance by the length of one of your feet on each side. Bend the knees until an angle of approximately ninety degrees is formed between the back of the calf and the back of the thigh. Keep the back straight, shoulders relaxed, and the buttocks tucked under.

THE UNICORN STANCE

(Chi Lin Bu)

This stance originated with the belief that a unicorn had to bend its knee in order to bow or to cleanse water. From this stance, the martial artist can move back easily and still have the ability to kick with the rear leg. (Like the unicorn, this posture allows the martial artist to avoid being caught unaware and unprepared.)

From the horse stance, place the right leg behind the left., bringing the knee of the right leg one inch above the ground and directly behind the left ankle (only go as far as is comfortable for you). The right leg is on its toes. The left foot is turned out, holding 80% of the body's weight. Reverse this process for the other leg.

CHAPTER 3

ADAPTATION FOR THE UNICORN STANCE

The movement from the horse stance to the unicorn stance is very significant, with mystical ties to Celtic mythology and astrology. The Celtic calendar was lunar and ripe with its own symbolism. Each of its 13 months was named for a particular tree whose character and spirit reflected specific qualities. Other symbols significant to each month reflected the various archetypal forces at play in the world during that month.

Two of the Celtic signs are associated with the summer solstice: The Oak (from June 10 to July 7) and The Holly (from July 8 to August 4). The summer solstice is one of the most powerful times of the year with many hidden significances. One of the more important is the time of the alchemical marriage, the blending of the male and female so that the Holy Child can be born.

We have already spoken briefly about the significance of the holly and its corresponding month, with the unicorn as one of its major symbols. The preceding month's tree is the oak and one of its primary symbols is the white horse, which was sacred and often an individual and tribal totem favorite Although horse cults existed prior to the arrival of the Celts, this animal became an important to Celtic tradition. In Welsh mythology, Rhiannon was the horse goddess.

The white horse of the oak month would evolve into the unicorn, a white horse with a single spiraling horn resembling a flaming spear, in the Celtic lunar calendar. These two trees of the summer solstice represent duality, male and female, solar and lunar, physical and spiritual, heaven and earth and our movement and work between them. Thus the white horse becomes the fabulous unicorn, making the use of these stances even more powerful and significant:

> These two trees, according to an ancient Welsh poem, formed two pillars of a bridge that spanned the "Rainbow River," which dissolved the evil violence of the world and flowed into the entrance of Gwynvyd.[7]

---

[7] Helena Paterson, *Handbook of Celtic Astrology* (St. Paul: Llewellyn Publications, 1994), p. 128.

TREASURES OF THE UNICORN

Gwynvyd is our equivalent of heaven, a place where one could unite with the divine and to which the Celts aspired to reach.

It is not difficult to use these stances to empower ourselves and our connection to the unicorn. Become familiar with the movements. Practice them. Take time to meditate upon the unicorn and its various correspondences. Visualize the unicorn as a companion wherever you go. Visualize the unicorn as coming more alive within you each time you focus upon it.

Do not become discouraged if you have difficulty maintaining these postures. In time, it will become easier, signaling how well you are aligning with the unicorn energy.

Performing this exercise at the beginning and end of the other exercises and meditations will further their empowerment. When performed at the beginning, they serve to shift the consciousness and the body's energy to be more in sync with the unicorn's.

When performed at the conclusion of other unicorn attunement work, assume the postures in their reverse order. Begin with the pose of the unicorn. Move from it to the horse stance. Then move from the horse stance to a relaxed standing posture. This further emphasizes the grounding, and shifts the consciousness back to the daily life.

In essence, you are moving into the unicorn energy, accessing it through the actual meditation, and then bringing it back out to manifest itself in your life. When performed at the end of meditation, these stances serve to shift back and ground the unicorn energy. This helps prevent the "spaciness" that can occur after some meditations.

Costumed Portion of Unicorn Dance

Build upon the basic unicorn stance. Incorporate costume and creative imagination into your own unicorn dance. Imbue your movements with significance. The more you do so, the more powerful the effect. The stronger your focus upon the unicorn, and seeing yourself as the unicorn, the stronger you will align with it's energies, manifesting more dynamically as a result.

1. Begin by standing straight. Relax. Close your eyes and take a few moments to breathe slowly.

2. Step into the horse stance. Keep your weight over your feet. Visualize yourself as a horse or astride a horse.

    •   Imagine the strength and energy of the horse coming alive within you. Imagine how you can apply this energy in your daily life.

    •   Hold this position for only a few minutes. Five is sufficient, or as long as you are comfortable. Until you get used to this posture, you may feel some discomfort.

        Stop if you do!

3. Move into the unicorn posture. Try to keep the movements smooth. Visualize yourself becoming one with the unicorn. See, feel, and imagine the unicorn's qualities coming alive within you. Imagine and feel your energy coming into attunement with that of the of the unicorn.

    •   Know that as you assume this posture the unicorn's energy is being invoked and will manifest itself in your life.

    •   Maintain this posture only as long as you are comfortable. No longer than five minutes is necessary.

        Stop if you feel any discomfort!

EXERCISE 4:

The Wondrous Horn

> **BENEFITS**
> - healing
> - purification
> - compassion
> - insight into healing methods
> - hope

Magickal storytelling is the use of stories, tales, and myths to expand perceptions, opening our minds to magickal states of consciousness. Ancient mystics and bards would imbue their tales with imagery to elicit dynamic effects, the stories reflecting and opening inner worlds.

Through storytelling, we can create a magickal journey, using the imagination in a concentrated and directed manner (in a relaxed, altered state of consciousness) to elicit specific responses in our own lives or the lives of our audience. Magickal storytelling activates greater inner energies and perceptions.

The imagination is one of our greatest assets and can be directed to enhance and augment our life. In our normal, daily life circumstances, this direction can achieved in a variety of ways besides magickal story telling: meditation, pathworking, guided journeys, and creative visualization provide ways to direct the imagination.

Stories, myths, and tales touch the core of humanity, opening us to the universal and timeless, bringing together the past, present, and future. Stories can build bridges between the physical and more subtle planes of life and stimulate and enhance initiation rites and higher consciousness exercises. Stories stir the creative imagination and open us up to new or forgotten possibilities.

Images within tales, when used in meditation or other magickal journeys, express and impress. Most tales are full of symbolism, enabling us to access deeper levels of mind and to awaken us to the unrecognized universal energies at play within our lives.

Throughout this book, stories will be used to open up more fully to the unicorn. The stories may change in the course of the meditation, but that's to be expected. Stories with archetypal energies grow and adapt to the individual's needs.

Magickal storytelling strengthens and deepens your perceptions of the unicorn, stimulates changes in your body and energy field that are softer and more compatible to the unicorn. Magickal storytelling increases reception to the feel and experience of the unicorn's energy, making you more responsive to the healing impact. Magickal storytelling helps you recognize transformations and use them most effectively, stimulating inspiration and creativity and making your dream life more vivid.

> **FRAGRANCES AND FLOWER ELIXIRS**
>
> apple blossom
> lilac
> clover
> orchid
> snapdragon
> lavender
> cedar
> violet

Magickal Storytelling Guidelines

Use aids to your meditation. Incenses, oils, and flower and gem elixirs can be beneficial. Many are particularly effective for any unicorn work. However, if you are performing the exercises outdoors, do not use fragrances.

1. Prepare ahead of time to assure you will not be disturbed or interrupted.

2. Magickal storytelling is especially effective performed outside. Wooded environments are best.

    *   If you do perform the exercises outdoors, meditating under an apple, cedar, oak, or especially a holly tree will greatly enhance the effectiveness.

    *   Choose a time and a place that is best for unicorn encounters.

3. Perform the unicorn postures to shift the mind away from the daily activities and to facilitate your own shifting of energies, increasing your receptiveness to the unicorn energy.

4. Make yourself comfortable. Perform a progressive relaxation. The more relaxed you are, the more receptive the unicorn becomes to you.

5. Read and familiarize yourself with the story.

    • You needn't memorize it, but you should be familiar enough with it to visualize the main events.

    • Throughout the exercise, visualize yourself as the main character to empower your connection to the unicorn.

6. Unless directed otherwise, use the same opening and closing scenarios in all of the meditations and exercises. The imagery has been chosen specifically to help you in your quest for the unicorn encounter.

7. At the end of the meditation, perform the unicorn stances in reverse order, grounding the energy, pulling it out of that ethereal mental realm, and releasing it to manifest itself in the physical realm.

    Remember that the meditation will elicit a physical manifestation, of which only a part will be building an invitation to an actual unicorn encounter.

8. Allow the story and its visualization to find its own level.

    • It will change.

    • It will take on a life of its own, a reflection of the unique relationship that you are building with the unicorn.

OPENING SCENARIO
(use for all exercises unless directed otherwise)

As your eyes close and you begin to relax, images begin to take shape within the mind. In the background, you hear the faint sound of a trickling stream and the soft splash of waterfalls. There is the sound of birds.

The Alicorn's Magic

The cooing of the mourning dove is clear and in the distance you hear the call of a peacock, a guardian of the unicorn.

You feel the grass, cool and damp with dew, beneath your feet. There is the smell of wild flowers and new mown hay. A soft breeze brushes across you, and there is a soft tinkling of chimes within it.

Above you the sun and moon share the sky, and you are not sure if it is dawn or dusk. Regardless, it is a quiet and powerful time. About you is an open meadow, encircled by ancient oaks and holly. The color of the wildflowers stand out against the rich green grass.

On the opposite end of this meadow is a small waterfall. The splash sends soft ripples into a glistening pool of water. From this pool, a stream issues forth and runs through the length of the meadow. Next to the pool is an apple tree. The pink and white blossoms cover the tree and the ground beneath it.

You breathe deeply of the sweet air as you walk slowly toward that pool. You are relaxed and at peace. You know this place. It is so familiar to you. You have seen it before, maybe in your dreams or maybe in a distant life time.

You seat yourself at the base of the apple tree. You gaze at surface of the crystalline pool of water. You can see your reflection upon its surface. The image is slightly distorted from the ripples created by the splash of the falls at the opposite end of the pool.

Then the water stills—in spite of the falls. The surface glistens like a mirror. The sun and moon are both reflected upon its surface and you see a soft glow about your own reflection. Then your image shimmers and disappears from the surface. As the water stills once more and you gaze softly upon it, you see new images rising from its depths and you feel yourself being drawn into them....

CHAPTER 3

MAGICKAL STORY:

THE WONDROUS HORN

(adapted from a Russian folktale,
"Katya and the Unicorn")

It had been a long, hot summer, hotter than usual. A drought had made water scarce. For some, there had only been enough water to drink. In these towns, no washing or wasting of water in any fashion was allowed. Because of this, dust and dirt covered the towns and their people. They were at a loss. No one knew what could be done.

Then people began to get sick. At first, those who were sick assumed it was because they were just dirty and tired. When the ill began to show rosy spots on different part of their body, panic set it. It had become worse. Typhoid!

The disease spread. The water source was contaminated. Men, women, and children began to die and panic filled peoples' hearts. Homes and clothing were set on fire. Still, the disease continued to spread. Some people hung herbs upon their doorways. Most prayed, but nothing seemed to help.

Times became more difficult and the people became desperate. They sought out their priests, who tried to exorcise the disease. Some sought out witches. Some turned to ancient gods and goddesses. Nothing helped. And still more people died.

Then someone suggested finding a unicorn. Although the people might have scoffed at such an idea before this time, only a few did so now. The alicorn was legendary for its healing.

Many people knew bits and pieces of unicorn legends, but no one was really sure how to find one. Where would they look? Didn't they need a virgin or a young woman with no husband or children? Didn't they have to trick it? Where would they start?

A young woman stepped forward. Her name was Katya, and she had worked hard to help those who were sick. She never worried over her own health. The only concern in her heart was for the well being of the others. As a child she had heard all the tales of the unicorn, and she had dreamed of them. She had never seen one, but she knew they lived. She did not know where, but her heart told her it was the only chance her family and her town had to survive.

"I will catch the unicorn," she told the townspeople.

"But you have a family and we need you here to help with the sick," the people replied. "You are not even close to being a virgin!"

"Unicorns trust and help those who help others, and unless we get some help, all of us will soon die. I know I am not perfect, but I must try to find one."

Ted Andrews

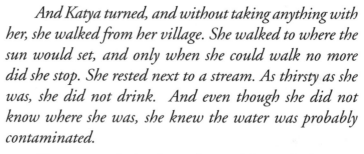

And Katya turned, and without taking anything with her, she walked from her village. She walked to where the sun would set, and only when she could walk no more did she stop. She rested next to a stream. As thirsty as she was, she did not drink. And even though she did not know where she was, she knew the water was probably contaminated.

She sat wondering how she would ever find a unicorn. She sat worrying over her family and friends, her hands resting in her lap. As the sun began to set, she heard a sound. As she looked up, on the other side of the stream was a magnificent unicorn! Its white coat glistened and the horn gave off a soft golden glow. As she looked at it, holding her breath, it fixed her with its blue eyes.

She felt all of her worry fade as she watched the unicorn touch its horn to the stream. The water bubbled and rippled, and the unicorn stood in the middle of it as all of the animals drew near to drink from the stream. Katya leaned forward and with her cupped hands brought the water to her mouth without hesitation. It was cool and sweet. Never had water tasted so good! And she drank her fill for the first time in months. She felt cleansed, purified, and free. She knew everything would be all right.

As Katya stood, the unicorn stepped back, but it met Katya's gaze. A minute passed and Katya felt her heart open and the unicorn knew her. The unicorn stepped forward and brought its nose to be touched by Katya. She was filled with joy and relief and awe! There was no doubt that the unicorn would follow her to the town.

As Katya led the unicorn back towards her town, they paused at every stream, pond, lake, and well. At each, the unicorn would dip its horn into the water. The water would bubble and swirl and be cleansed. It became pure once more!

The people stood in awe as Katya led the unicorn through the town. She took it to every house. The magnificent creature held its horn over those who were ill. They felt better at once.

At dawn, Katya led the unicorn back to the edge of town to say good-bye and thanks. A crowd gathered. Someone in the crowd whispered, "What if the sickness comes back?"

Others whispered in response, "Maybe we should keep the horn. That is where the magic lies."

And yet another said, "But that would mean killing it."

Though the words were soft whispers, they roared like thunder in the unicorn's ears. It squealed, rearing up, and before anyone could move, it had disappeared from sight. Katya looked to the direction of the whispers in horror, accusing with her eyes. She knew in that moment she could not live in a town that harbored such thoughts.

Katya and her family left the town to follow the unicorn.

And when sickness came again to that town, no unicorn came.

Nor ever would again.

CHAPTER 3

CLOSING SCENARIO

The images of the story fade, and you see your own reflection within that pool of water once more. Then you see the image of a unicorn overlaying your own. You catch your breath, and as you raise your eyes from the pool's surface, on the opposite side stands that magnificent creature. Its eyes meet your gaze, and in that moment your heart opens and you are filled with tremendous love. Then, before you can blink, the unicorn turns and disappears from your view.

You look to the surface of the pool once more and you still see the unicorn's image overlaying your own. Then the scenario slowly fades, and you find yourself shifting from the inner back into the outer—healed, blessed, and filled with great hope and expectation!

Unicorns in Moonlight

CHAPTER 4

The Eastern Unicorn

Like a lion without fear of the howling pack,
Like a gust of wind, never trapped in a snare.
Like a lotus blossom, never sprinkled by water.
Like me, like a unicorn, in solitude roam.

Hymn of Buddha

Before creation, the universe was merely an egg. Heaven and earth were together. The stars and the planets were one. But all eggs hatch, and when the egg of the universe cracked, chaos spilled out. Heaven and earth separated. The stars and the planets split.

In an ancient Chinese creation myth, it took P'an Ku, the first god/human, 18,000 years to create our present universe and earth from that chaos. He was assisted in this by the four most fortunate animals—the dragon, the phoenix, the tortoise and the unicorn.

The Four Sacred Beasts

When P'an Ku was done, he died. The dragon swam into the seas. The tortoise crawled into the swampy wetlands. The phoenix took to the sky and flew to the open lands. The unicorn galloped into the green forests. These four animals became the guardians to the hidden realms upon the earth and those places beyond, and their strength is undiminished by contact with humans.

In the East, the unicorn is more ancient than those records of it within the western world. There are many more tales of unicorn miracles and wonders than there ever were in the West. China, Japan, Korea, and Vietnam all had tales and teachings of the unicorn. In parts of the Middle East (ancient Persia. Iran, Iraq, and Arabia), there arose great tales

Ch'i Lin

of the unicorn as well. In China the unicorn was called *Ch'i Lin* or *K'i Lin*. In Japan it was known as the *Kirin* or *Sin-you*. In Persia, it was called *Karkadann*.

1. DRAGON

sleeps within the sea but can fly to the heavens; goodness and power flow to all nearby; can change one's fate; and controls the climate—of the earth or of one's life

2. PHOENIX

the dragon's wife; helps the dragon right wrongs; considerate of all living things; always attended to by a small train of birds; most beautiful and virtuous; waits for peace to return to the earth

3. TORTOISE

gives power and strength to humans enduring difficulties; strong, wise, and kind; always considered a female and can only mate with snakes; assists those going through changes and transitions

4. UNICORN

always gaily colored; symbol of luck; long life and joy are born from its appearance; brings and awakens justice and law; a sign of illustrious offspring

Although quite different in appearance than the western unicorn, the eastern unicorn shared many of its wondrous characteristics. The eastern unicorn, for example, was a solitary animal. In Eastern tradition, the unicorn sprang from the center of the earth, the first and most perfect of the 360 land creatures. The unicorn's gentleness prevented it from treading upon an insect or eating fruit. It was so sensitive it could feel the weight of a shadow cast by the light of the moon. All animals became tame around it. Fire and rain did the unicorn's bidding, and when it plucked a leaf, two more grew in its place. The voice was sweet and delicate, with the sound of a thousand wind chimes.

The eastern unicorn always reaches its destination, never falling into pits or traps, so was honored as a great spiritual guide through life. In the East, there arose a belief that once the unicorn was tamed, no other animal would ever know terror again. As long as humans displayed greed, anger, and war, and hunger was about, the unicorn would remain hidden, wild, and reclusive.

The Ch'i Lin surfaces in unexpected places of modern China. Above is a depiction of the Ch'i Lin in the heraldry of the University of Hong Kong.

During evil times, it appears only when a great change is about to occur.

In China, the Ch'i Lin has a multicolored body and is an animal of great power and wisdom, walking so softly its hooves make no sound. It is so soft hearted it does not want to crush the blades of grass beneath its feet. Avoiding fighting at all costs, its voice sounds like a thousand wind chimes and it can live for 1000 years.

CHAPTER 4

The unicorn of the East is occasionally linked with the tiger and the lioness. Although not always a compatible relationship in Western lore, in the East it is. The tiger is a fierce, grand creature in Eastern tradition, its courage and ferocity often unmatched. The tiger is considered a yang (male) creature, as opposed to the yin (female) unicorn and fights the earthly demons which encourage humans to kill the Ch'i Lin. Lion and lioness are very similar, fighting for wisdom and truth and scaring away demons with tooth and claw.

Japan's version of the unicorn, the *Kirin* or *Sin-you*, had more of a lion's sinew. Although the Kirin was normally shy and would take large detours to avoid confrontations, the Sin-you unicorn was not so timid. Noted for its ability to know right from wrong, it was often called upon to determine guilt. If an individual were guilty, the Sin-you would fix its eyes upon him and pierce the guilty person with its horn.

In Taoism and other mystical Eastern traditions, there rose a variety of teachings in art and dance to honor all of nature, and this included the unicorn and all sacred beasts. In Vietnam, a yearly unicorn dance is held on the full moon of the eighth month, the time when all of creation holds its breath in anticipation of the monsoon season. People put on masks and costumes to conceal their identity. When their spirits are high, they tie an effigy of the unicorn to a platform. Archers then shoot at it while singing the effigy song shown in the sidebar. After the song, the rains would begin.

The unicorn, as with other sacred beasts and with most animals of nature, became the basis of martial arts forms, healing techniques, sexual positions, and dances. These physical movements served to invoke the energy of the creature more strongly, as we discussed briefly in the previous chapter. More intricate dances, along with some of

---

EFFIGY SONG

The unicorn's hoofs!
The duke's sons throng.
Alas for the unicorn!

The unicorn's brow!
The duke's kinsmen throng.
Alas for the unicorn!

The unicorn's horn!
The duke's clansmen throng.
Alas for the unicorn![1]

---

their applications, will be examined more fully in an exercise at the end of this chapter.

The Ch'i Lin shows itself at particular times. When a ruler is just and kind and the times peaceful and prosperous, the unicorn will appear in a glade as a sign of good fortune. It will also appear in a similar location when a great leader is about to be born or die. The Ch'i Lin appeared to the mother of Confucius.

Approximately 2500 years ago, during the Chou dynasty, a young woman by the name of Yen Ching-tsai made a visit to a temple. While praying in the temple, she went into a trance and five men appeared before her. The air about them shimmered like water and was filled with the scent of cinnamon. The five men led a strange looking animal, the Ch'i Lin. It stepped forward and nuzzled her hand. A tiny jade tablet dropped into her hand. As he nuzzled her hand, the Ch'i Lin pulled a ribbon from her hair. On one side of the jade tablet was a message similar to the following:

> The son of the essence of water shall succeed to the withering Chou and he will become a throneless king.

The young Yen Ching-tsai, the "essence of water," would give birth to K'ung Fu-tze, or Confucius. In yet another version, the mother of Confucius was walking with two maids when the Ch'i Lin appeared. She took a fine ribbon from her hair and hung it over its horn and the creature became calm and contented. It walked about her three times and then disappeared. Eleven months after this encounter, Confucius was born.

Many of the great leaders of the East were associated with the unicorn, including Confucius, Genghis Khan, and Huang Ti (The Yellow Emperor), the mythical first emperor of China. He developed the calendar, was considered the first builder of houses, initiated the higher metamorphosis of China's state of being, and came to symbolize fame, progress, and advancement.

CHAPTER 4

The emperor Fu Hsi saw the magical Ch'i Lin across the Yellow River. It had the scales of a dragon and a silver horn. As Fu Hsi watched, muddy waters became as clear as glass wherever the unicorn stopped, and it left a trail of emeralds wherever it walked.

The unicorn stood in front of Fu Hsi and stomped its foot three times. Its back was covered with strange writings and magical signs and symbols.

THE CH'I LIN
AND
THE GIRAFFE

*The giraffe was mistaken for a unicorn
by Chinese explorers in Africa.*

Fu Hsi reported that the unicorn's voice was like a monastery bell, and the writings on its back would become the first written language of China. Fu Hsi would also introduce musical instruments and the trigrams of the mysterious I Ching into the Chinese culture.

By the Middle Ages, most of the people in China were very familiar with the unicorn, and some of the reports of its appearance had an unusual and often humorous aspect. When Chinese sailors reached East Africa in 1415, they heard stories of the horned creature that they knew of as the Ch'i Lin and were surprised because Africa was so different from China.

The Africans spoke of an animal with the body of a deer, a long neck and a single horn. It was graceful, gentle, and seldom spoke or made noises, and was reported to be 18 feet tall. It was also given to hiding among the mimosa. This African unicorn turned out to be the giraffe.

The Middle Eastern Unicorn

In Persia and Arabia, the unicorn took the form of the ferocious *Karkadann.* This animal was so fierce it could even attack and kill an elephant. In fact, only the dove could tame it. The Karkadann responded so strongly to the dove's gentle call, the beast would lie beneath the dove's tree for hours. Under the nest of the dove, the Karkadann would wait for the dove to light upon its horn.

The Karkadann was a violent, warlike unicorn, born in blood and vehement in battle. It had the body of a rhino and a tail like a lion. Each leg had three hooves, one in front and two in back. From its forehead rose a single black horn, curved like a crescent. Unlike the western unicorn, it was dreaded by all living creatures and left alone.

In other descriptions, it was a fierce but magical animal. It resembled a stag, horse, or antelope, and the elephant was its deadly enemy. It could be mild and tender hearted though, drinking the morning dew from green plants. When it put its head in water, the water would become pure and fruitful. Opposites would unite, and all female creatures in that water would become pregnant. The evil within the water would die and be cast out upon the shore. The Karkadann could also join that which was separate, and in its presence, humans meet their own shadows face to face.

The Karkadann was extremely fond of women. In fact, women, as they were in the west, used as lures. However, in the eastern tradition, the women did not have to be virgins. The Karkadann would approach a woman, nuzzle her hand and then unbind her breasts, licking and suckling them. If the woman were lactating, the breast milk would make the Karkadann drunk. Capture of this unicorn was even rarer than in the western tradition since it was difficult to find women willing to cooperate.

The elephant was the deadly enemy of the Karkadann. Many tales report of their great battles. In the most famous of these tales, the Karkadann stabs the elephant in the belly with its horn, but could not dislodge it and the elephant then collapses upon the Karkadann. The giant mythical bird of Persia, the Roc, flies by at this moment, diving and grabbing both and lifting them up to the sky. The Roc flies to its nest and feeds both the Karkadann and the elephant to its young.

In tales such as this, it is not difficult to see the symbolism in the union of opposites, part of the meaning of this Middle Eastern unicorn. Those who are into animal totems and drawn to the unicorn are likely to have the elephant as a totem as well. A study of the characteristics of the elephant may be beneficial. There are a lot of similarities between elephants and unicorns. Although elephants have two tusks, the most outstanding characteristic is the long trunk from the middle of its head. It has mystical ties to the power of the libido. The elephant has great sensitivity and a strong feeling nature, and like the unicorn, is connected to ancient wisdom and power.

Only one human has truly ever tamed the Karkadann—Iskandar or Alexander the Great. In his conquests of the world, he rode upon the Karkadann named Bucephalus, described in tales as having the body of a horse and the head of a lion. Alexander the Great, as reported in tales, spoke softly to him, stroked him, and leaned against him. Bucephalus was fearless against demons and allowed Alexander to tame griffins.

Whether in the Far East or the Middle East, the unicorn was mysterious and magical. Even in these distant places, it had great connections to the creatures and beings of the supernatural world—what we call the Faerie Realm—as well as the natural world.

Notes

CHAPTER 4

EXERCISE 5:   Dances of the Sacred Beasts

BENEFITS
- strengthens relationships
- open doors to inner realm
- healing
- power
- animal communication

The four sacred beasts—the dragon, the phoenix, the tortoise, and the unicorn—have a unique relationship. All serve as guardians and protectors to the earth's animals, to nature in general, and the hidden realms we have access to while upon this planet. In the East, these animals are steeped in great mysticism, magic, and power. They are companions to each other, so when you develop a relationship with one, you are also establishing subtle, but real connections with the others as well.

As mentioned previously, most animals have had dances associated with them as a way of aligning with and invoking their energy and essence. These dances had many healing and magical applications and also included those creatures most think of as mythical or fantastic. The movements and postures of creatures, real and fantastic, became a source of great power in the East. These movements were incorporated into the martial arts, spiritual dances, celebrations, sexual activities, and a variety of mystical healing practices.

In Exercise 3 in the previous chapter, I provided guidelines for the unicorn stance. In this exercise you will use the unicorn posture along with the postures for the other three sacred beasts. Performing all four movements together becomes a dance of spiritual relationships, strengthening healing of the entire body, eliminating blockages and freeing up energy, and helping to open all aspects of the natural world. In addition, the combination of movements can assist work with animals, especially in understanding their communications.

1. Make all preliminary preparations.

    *   Perform these movements outside as a prelude to any work in nature, whether gardening or animal communications, will encourage the success of the work with nature.

    *   Take time to focus and meditate upon the qualities and characteristics of each of the sacred beasts.

        Dragon = power, strength, change of fortune, blessing, protection

        Phoenix = rebirth, beauty, dream flights, virtue, righting of wrongs

        Tortoise = endurance, strength, wisdom and kindness

2. Visualize yourself as the sacred creature as you perform each movement.

    *   Know and feel the creature's energy and essence coming alive within you.

    *   Sometimes it helps to visualize all that you can accomplish by aligning with their energy.

3. Begin by standing straight. Relax, close your eyes, and breathe regularly. Open your eyes.

4. Perform the unicorn postures, moving from the horse stance to the unicorn pose as described in Chapter 3, Exercise 3.

    *   See and feel yourself becoming the unicorn. Hold this pose, envisioning everything it means for you.

    *   See the energy of the unicorn becoming more alive for you within your day-to-day life.

5. Pause. Rise from the unicorn stance, and move into the dragon pose illustrated here. Perform the dragon posture to the right and to the left.

    - See and feel yourself becoming the dragon.

    - See and feel its energy coming alive for you and within you.

    - See and feel the dragon touching your life.

THE DRAGON POSE

The flying dragon pose will instill the characteristics of the dragon into the mind and body. It is good to see oneself flying while holding this position. In healing, it brings equilibrium to the heart. It should be performed to the right and to the left. Repeat three times (right, left, right, left, right, left). Keep the movements slow and steady.

6. Pause. Rise from the dragon pose and move into the phoenix pose illustrated here.

    •   See and feel yourself becoming the phoenix.

    •   See and feel its energies of rebirth awakening within your life.

    •   Imagine all that is manifesting for you as a result of this exercise, holding the pose and visualizing all that it represents for you.

THE PHOENIX POSE

Raise the arms sideways to shoulder level, palms down. The right knee is raised at the same time, while the left heel is lifted off the floor. Then lower the arms and legs back down. Repeat. Raise the arms up, but this time, the left knee is lifted and the right heel is off the ground. Repeat the entire cycle three times (right, left, right, left, right, left). Keep your movements slow and smooth. Imagine yourself as the phoenix rising from the ashes and taking flight through infinite space. See your life moving forward.

7. Pause. Move from the posture of the phoenix to the tortoise posture.

- See and feel the strength and power of the tortoise coming alive within your life.

- See and feel its energy manifesting as you see and feel yourself as the tortoise, holding the pose and visualizing all that it represents for you.

THE TORTOISE POSE

This may be performed sitting or standing. Bring your chin down to your chest. At the same time stretch the top of your head. The back of the neck will feel an upward pull and the shoulders will relax downward. Inhale as you perform this action. Slowly bring the back of the skull down as if to touch the back of the neck. Your chin is pulled upward and your throat is slightly stretched. Exhale as you perform this. Perform this slowly. See and feel yourself as the tortoise, extending its head from its shell and then drawing it back in.

8. Move from the tortoise posture back to the unicorn's.

   • See and feel the unicorn's energy alive within your life.

   • See and feel all that it represents for you, holding the pose and visualizing yourself as the living unicorn.

9. Move from the unicorn posture into the horse's stance.

   • This will ground the energy you have activated and anchor its manifestation into the physical world in which you operate daily.

   • Some find it beneficial to visualize the horse leading them into the inner realms at the beginning and then leading them out at the end. In this way, the series of movements become a journey in and out of those ethereal realms.

10. Stand straight and relax. Breathe deeply and evenly. Feel your feet solid and parallel upon the ground. You are connected to the earth more strongly than ever before.

    • Take a moment and visualize everything about your life and your relationships strengthened.

    • See and feel the energy of all the sacred creatures strong within you, all in great harmony with each other.

    • Know that this harmony extends to all relationships in the outer world, making them stronger and more harmonious.

CHAPTER 4

<u>EXERCISE 6:</u> **Council of Imaginary Beasts**

<table>
<tr><td>

BENEFITS
* attunement with nature
* renewed sense of wonder
* vibrant dream activity
* general balance

</td></tr>
</table>

Many legends speak of a time when the Earth was watched over by what many now call imaginary beasts: the dragon, the phoenix, the unicorn, the tortoise, the griffin, and other fantastic creatures. These creatures were born at the beginning of time. Each had its own task, and each worked with the others guarding all life upon the planet, keepers of the realm of mystery and imagination. As long as they live within our imaginations, our stories and our dreams, they will be found somewhere within the world.

These fantastic creatures should always be approached from several perspectives. They should be recognized as life forms of their own, with all of their own unique characteristics. They can also be viewed as archetypal forces within nature and within the lives of humans, giving power to their symbolic significance as well.

No matter what the imaginary creature may be, every detail of it should be noted. The color, the size, the temperament and behaviors should always be examined in relation to you and some aspect of your life. The more you understand these aspects, the greater the creature's power to affect you. Even something as simple as focusing upon them in meditation activates a play of their energy somewhere in your life.

Focusing upon the imaginary beasts also serves to awaken and strengthen our own imaginative faculties. This exercise will help in that awakening. I have found this exercise to be effective in many ways. Sometimes I use it before taking nature walks, helping to attune to nature and all its inhabitants—plant, animal, and spiritual. This exercise can also be used just as a general "tonic meditation." It heals, awakening a renewed sense of joy and wonder at the world and life in general. It can also be used to stimulate the creative fires. Performing this exercise before bedtime can stimulate vibrant dream activity. Most importantly, it opens the door to actual encounters.

The Eastern Unicorn

The fantastic creatures are rare and reclusive and do not readily reveal themselves, although their energies can be felt and experienced. Exercises such as this manifest these energies somewhere in your life.

As with all meditations, it is good to make preliminary preparations. In general, with any meditation it is best to remove any possibility of interruption. Make sure you will be undisturbed. Next, it is beneficial to make sure that you are relaxed. Performing a progressive relaxation can be of great benefit. Send warm, soothing sensations to every part of your body. Start at the feet and work your way upward. Take your time with this. The more relaxed you are, the more effective the exercise.

1. To enhance the effectiveness of this exercise, begin by performing the dances of the sacred beasts. Begin with the unicorn, and move to the dragon, the phoenix and the tortoise. This will help the mind shift and help you align your energies.

2. For this exercise, you will use the Opening Scenario described in Chapter 3, Exercise 4. Relax and allow the image of that wondrous meadow to begin to unfold within your mind.

   • See yourself sitting beside that crystalline pool of water. Your reflection is clear upon the surface, and the soft splash of the waterfall is soothing.

   • Butterflies flutter about, and a breeze gently brushes across your face and body. As it does, you hear the soft tinkling of silver bells. You raise your eyes from the pool's surface and look across to the other side. You breathe deeply, and allow the scenario following Step 3 to unfold.

3. After the completion of the scenario's unfolding, to further ground this energy and set the effects in motion more dynamically, follow the scenario up with the dances for the sacred beasts again.

   • Perform them in reverse order. Begin with the tortoise, move to the phoenix and then on to the dragon.

   • Conclude with the unicorn, moving from the unicorn stance to the horse stance to normal posture.

CHAPTER 4

SCENARIO

There, as if appearing from nowhere, stands that magnificent unicorn. It seems to shine with a silver glow, and the deep eyes hold you fixed. The golden spiral rising from the center of its forehead catches and reflects the sunlight.

Your heart sings in its presence, and you know that its appearance heralds something special. It seems to smile as if reading your thoughts. It lowers its head and dips its alicorn into the water.

The water begins to swirl and bubble. A spiraling spout of water rises from the center of the pool, extending itself to the sky. As the sunlight hits the spiral of water, rainbow hues become visible within it. Still it extends higher. Then the spout erupts, sending a soft spray over you and the meadow around you.

As you wipe the spray from your eyes, you catch your breath. The spout of water is gone, but filling the sky is a magnificent dragon. The energy rolls off of it in waves, like the heat off the pavement on a hot summer's day. You look across to the unicorn, and its eyes remove any fear that you have in the presence of such primal power.

As the dragon soars above, the sky shifts, and you see the shifting of the climate about you. You are awe struck as the dragon's ability to affect the weather with the subtlest movements. Then it hovers directly above you. You see that the dragon holds within its claws a great pearl. It releases the pearl and it drifts down toward you as gently as a soap bubble. You catch the pearl, cupping it within both hands. As you do, you hear the dragon's words strong within your mind.

"When you awaken and draw upon your true essence, the climate of your life will change. Troublesome elements of life will not interfere. That which did not work before will now do so. With this, I will help. I will show you the power you have to change the climate—the fortune—of your life. And I will help to smooth the way."

Your hands begin to tingle as the pearl begins to pour forth energy into you. It fills you, strengthens you. It has been a long time since you felt such strength and control. Your confidence grows, and doubts begin to dissipate. As you gaze upon that pearl within your hands, you see your life path opening. You see images of opportunities presenting themselves to you in the days ahead. And you realize that you have the ability to change any aspect of your life that you desire.

Then the pearl begins to glow, the light emanating from it growing stronger and brighter, and you find yourself squinting. Its shine becomes even more intense. As you watch, the pearl melts in your hand with a final flash of brilliance. The light fades, your eyes begin to readjust, your hands are still cupped in front of you—empty.

The dragon is gone. The pearl is gone. You are sitting beside the pool of water. You are stunned. Your eyes look across the pool toward the unicorn, and it holds your gaze for only a moment. Then a second time it dips its horn into the water and a flame rises from its center.

The flame extends upward, shifting and stretching, rising high into the air above the pool. There it forms itself into the mythical bird of rebirth—the golden phoenix. As your eyes fix upon the phoenix, its plumage shimmers, changing colors, each more brilliant than the one before. One of those feathers drifts down and lands softly upon your lap. As you take the feather within your hands, you hear the soft voice of the phoenix within your mind.

"Life is change. It is a series of deaths and rebirths. I am your mirror. Just as I rise from the ashes, so do you from the ashes of every life experience. As you begin to recognize me within your life, you will find what you thought had died. The dreams you thought had died will be reborn, for dreams are never lost—merely forgotten."

CHAPTER 4

As you hold the feather, you close your eyes, remembering all of the dreams you had given up or refused to follow. You feel a soft warmth filling you like a fire coming to life within you, and there is no doubt that the opportunities to pursue the dreams you now hold dearest will present themselves yet again in the days ahead. You see yourself clearly following and capturing those dreams. You see the opportunities to make them a reality manifesting within your life.

As you open your eyes, the phoenix is gone— as is the feather you held within your hands. You are sitting still beside that crystalline pool. The unicorn stands on the opposite side. Watching all that is going on within your heart.

A third time the unicorn touches its alicorn to the water. A ripple surfaces in the middle and moves in your direction. As it splashes the pool's edge in front of you, you shift back a little. Then you realize you are not alone. Beside you rests a large tortoise, and as you notice it, it pushes its head forward out of the shell and fixes you with its eyes. In that moment you realize the tortoise has been with you from the beginning. It had remained so still you had been unaware of its presence. Gently you reach out and place your hand upon its shell, and you hear its voice within your mind.

"Life's tasks become easier when we find joy in the little things and when we learn to use the stillness. Permanent progress occurs one step at a time. A seed cannot be forced to grow. It must germinate, take root, sprout, and then blossom. Each stage is as important and as creative as the one which came before and the one which follows. When you learn to live in the moment, to be still within yourself in that moment, all doors will open. You are then at your most creative, for every moment has its own dynamic sparks. There is a time to stay within and a time to move out. This I will teach you to see. Every moment and every person, then, becomes an opportunity to manifest your creativity."

As you look down upon the tortoise, the markings on the back begin to shift and blend. New images arise. You see the times when you tried to rush or force growth, only to see things collapse or be delayed. You see the times in which you allowed events to unfold themselves and the success that occurred. As the images fade, you realize life is supposed to work out. You realize it always will if we do what we must and then allow it to take its own course.

Then you notice the tortoise is gone. You stand and you gaze upon the unicorn who has introduced you to these ancient friends. Your heart is filled with love and thanks for these reminders. A soft breeze brushes across you in response to your thoughts. The sound of silver bells surrounds you, and the pool begins to ripple and bubble before you. As you gaze into the pool, it stills.

Your reflection is clear upon its surface. Surrounding you in that reflection are the wise counselors and guardians—the dragon, the phoenix, the tortoise, and especially the unicorn. You are filled with a sense of wonder and you realize you are never alone. This thought itself is a promise of new joys about to unfold.

CLOSING SCENARIO

Then the water begins to ripple yet again, and the images begin to distort and fade, as does the meadow about you. You breathe deeply, feeling more grounded and with a stronger sense of promise to your life than you have felt in ages.

CHAPTER 4

<u>EXERCISE 7</u>: **Genghis Khan and the Unicorn**

<table>
<tr><td>

BENEFITS

- spirit contact
- life path guidance and clarity
- clarity in decisions
- recognizing signs and omens

</td></tr>
</table>

Part of what the unicorn teaches us is to pay closer attention to our inner prompting. Aligning with the unicorn's energy makes us more sensitive to the natural flow and rhythms of life. Heeding those rhythms is often difficult for people in the modern world. Most have been programmed to ignore anything but the rational. The unicorn helps us to reconnect with our more sensitive and intuitive side, enabling us to recognize many of the subtleties of life, including the presence of spirit.

Nature speaks to us all of the time, but in our modern world we have forgotten how to listen to it. We have not been taught its language. The unicorn is one of the guardians of the natural world, and thus speaks all of the languages of nature. By working with the unicorn, we open more fully to those languages and begin to see the signs, omens, and communications nature gives us every day. We begin to see patterns, and thus we can make choices and decisions that are more productive for ourselves.

This magickal storytelling is wonderfully effective for becoming more sensitive to spirit contact. When I have led groups through this exercise, it is common for many to experience the presence of deceased loved ones in the days following. Their presence may be detected in a variety of ways. There may be a familiar fragrance. Some individuals have seen them and even heard their voice calling to them. For others, like Genghis Kahn in this story, there is an overwhelming familiar feeling of the individual's presence.

This exercise will also help you to see more clearly the patterns and choices within your life. It is not uncommon for individuals making major decisions in their life to find that certain options are eliminated after performing this exercise, making the decisions easier. Sometimes within a day or two, the individual comes into possession of new information that facilitates the decision-making process.

1. Use the Opening and Closing Scenarios described in Chapter 3, Exercise 4.

2. Make all of the preliminary preparations.

3. Perform the unicorn stances, and remember to visualize yourself in the role of Genghis Kahn.

   • Although he was about to march upon India in the story, do not be afraid to substitute one of choices in its place.

   • You will be surprised at the illumination that comes to you about your goal in the days following this exercise.

MAGICKAL STORY:

GENGHIS KAHN AND THE UNICORN

Genghis Kahn was one of the most powerful rulers of China. Considered by many as a cruel barbarian, he embraced the heartless image. Regardless of the perception of him, his ability as a leader was highly respected. Although his methods may have been cruel, they were most successful. He acquired an empire that stretched from Korea to Persia, and yet he was never satisfied. There was always something more to conquer, to possess. His hunger and desire seemed undying. He wanted the world.

Few knew how deep his feelings were for his family. His father was especially important to his life. For most people, there are catalytic events in life. For Khan, it was his father's death. Kahn's quest for power grew stronger than ever after his father's death, and many believed Kahn was fulfilling a promise he once made to his father. Before each battle, he would ask for the guidance of his father in the great task ahead.

In 1224, Khan's army marched toward India. No one could stop him. No one dared to stop him. He con-

quered town and city, his armies marching over mountain after mountain, moving closer to his next great victory. He reached the last mountain and he was ready to conquer India.

He arose before the sun, climbing to the top of that last mountain to view and assess the coming battle. As he reached the top, he stopped in amazement. There was no army to meet his. There were no soldiers at all. There was only the morning sun beginning to rise.

As he stood atop the mountain, confused that no resistance was to be given, his eyes widened and he gasped. From behind a large boulder stepped a strange beast. It was small, about the size of a young deer. It was green, and it had a single horn of red and black protruding from its forehead.

Kahn stood motionless. What could this mean? He knew this beast. He knew it was the Ch'i Lin, the unicorn because he had heard many legends and tales about it. Although he knew it could speak many languages, the Ch'i Lin said not a word as it walked slowly toward him. It stopped three feet in front of him, its eyes locked upon his own.

Then this small animal knelt three times at Khan's feet. The air about began to shimmer. A strange fragrance—one he had not experienced in a very long time—enveloped him. Khan began to tremble. For the first time in his life, Khan felt fear.

He looked into the eyes of the unicorn, and the eyes began to change. A strange familiar feeling crept over Khan. It was a feeling Khan had when his father was alive. As he looked upon the unicorn, he realized the eyes of his father were gazing at him from the unicorn's eyes. Khan was truly afraid now, for it had been years since his father had died.

This had to be a sign!

Then he heard his father's voice strong within his head. It was as clear as if his father were standing right next to him. Khan could hear faintly in the distance his own army growing restless for Khan's signal to begin the battle, but he did not move. The air grew clear and still around him once more. The fragrance he had always associated with his father faded, and the eyes of the unicorn became its own again.

Khan turned slowly away from the unicorn and looked out at the expanse of his army below. A hush fell over them, waiting to hear Khan's words. He closed his eyes for a moment and then spoke loud and clear. His voice touched every ear in the morning air.

"Turn back!" he said. "My father has warned me not to go on!"

He then turned his back to the army and looked once more upon the strange creature before him. Tears filled his eyes. The unicorn lifted its head and was gone.

Notes

CHAPTER 5

The Lion and the Unicorn

The lion and the unicorn
Were fighting for the crown.
The lion chased the unicorn
All around the town.

English Nursery Rhyme

The Lion and the Unicorn

From the 12th century on, reports of the unicorn's appearance increased, and by the 16th century the unicorn was known and recognized throughout Europe. Most reports were hearsay, but during medieval times they achieved their greatest popularity.

In the 15th century, the unicorn image began to appear in all varieties of art, illustrating altars and prayer books, carved into doorways and wooden chests, painted and woven into tapestries. The story of "The Lady and the Unicorn" which introduces this chapter is from a tapestry at the Cluny Museum in Paris.

The unicorn's beauty, strength, and power began to take on profound meaning and overtones, both physical and spiritual, for the general public. Any depiction of it was presumed to be a link to its power. Its image became more horselike, an animal of purity and grace, with snowy white flanks and a horn of mother-of-pearl. It had a silken beard and was accompanied by the scent of apple blossoms and cinnamon. It was as swift as thought, and only the loveliest and most pure maidens could approach it. The unicorn became a common symbol both for maidens and for Christ and was always a symbol of new beginnings.

Throughout the unicorn's history, the lion has been linked to it in some fashion. The unicorn is the purest of all animals, and the lion was considered the most majestic. The two began to appear in stories, songs, and myths. In most, they are fighting or play-

> ### A UNICORN FOLK SONG
>
> (Often songs and poems using unicorn imagery would surface during the Middle Ages. It became a common image, particularly in romantic pieces. The following is a medieval German folk song.)
>
> *The hunter stood beside me*
> *Who blew the mighty horn;*
> *I saw that he was hunting*
> *The gentle unicorn—*
> *But the unicorn is noble,*
> *He knows his gentle birth*
> *He knows that God has chosen him*
> *Above all beasts on earth.*
>
> *The unicorn is noble;*
> *He keeps him safe and high*
> *Upon a narrow path and steep*
> *Climbing to the sky;*
> *And there no man can take him,*
> *He scorns the hunter's dart,*
> *And only a virgin's magic power*
> *Shall tame his haughty heart.*[1]

---

[1] James Cross Giblin, *The Truth About Unicorns* (New York: Harper Collins, 1991), p. 1.

ing, but even when playing, the stories often end in disaster. As far back as 3500 BC, a fight between these two animals is depicted on a Chaldean checkerboard.[2] In Babylonia, there is a story of a battle between a lion and a one-horned beast. Mycenean coins, artifacts, and Babylonian seals depict them. To some scholars, the lion stands for summer, the unicorn for spring. Thus, every year the lion triumphs over the unicorn, but the unicorn is forever reborn to fight another day.

THE UNICORN
AND THE LION

The Royal Arms of Her Majesty Queen Elizabeth II, borne by each monarch since Queen Victoria. The unicorn and the lion together share the support.

During the Middle Ages, new legends and associations arose surrounding the unicorn and even the lion In Europe, these stories reflected the old wars between England and Scotland. Before peace came between them, the supporters of the Royal Arms of Scotland had been two unicorns; the English adopted any beasts that took their fancy

Robert III of Scotland (1390) ruled with violence and fear during a period when Scotland continually fought with England. In his latter years, he became despondent and desired peace and prosperity between England and Scotland. He realized peace would only come through the strength and virtue provided by the unicorn, and it would not come for several centuries.

In 1567, Mary, Queen of Scots abdicated, and her son became James VI of Scotland. In 1603 when Elizabeth I of England died, James VI ascended to the throne as James I of England. He took the Scottish unicorn to England where it first shared the support of the Royal Arms with the English lion. In 1707, Scotland and England were officially united. Even today, these combined images still support the royal arms of Great Britain.

---

[2] Robin Palmer, *Dragons, Unicorns & Other Magical Beasts* (New York: Henry Walck, Inc., 1966), p. 121.

TREASURES OF THE UNICORN

Throughout the Middle Ages, these two animals would often appear together in heraldry, be it the heraldry of a country or of a family. Even the coat of arms for the Andrews family has a rampant lion and a rampant unicorn. Although the relationship was not always amicable, the unicorn and the lion together represented a formidable force—spiritual and otherwise.

The Medieval Fighting Unicorn

Although the unicorn's association with the lion was commonly recognized, during medieval times, the focus was still primarily upon the unicorn. As the public's fascination with the unicorn grew, the perception of its qualities and characteristics began to undergo subtle changes. It was still recognized as an animal with wondrous healing abilities, but in people's perception, the unicorn also grew wilder. In Grimm's tale of "The Brave Tailor," the king sends the tailor out to rid his forest of a unicorn said to be destroying the woods. The tailor lures the unicorn into charging, but the unicorn thrusts its horn into a tree. Stuck, the unicorn is at the mercy of the tailor, who promptly cuts off its horn and with a rope, leads the now docile unicorn back to the king.

In another version of this story, the lion and the unicorn chase across heaven and earth fighting. The unicorn's stamina is too great for the lion, the lion tires, and the unicorn bears down upon him. At the last moment, the lion leaps behind a tree. The unicorn, moving too fast to stop, thrusts its horn through the tree, and becomes stuck. The lion then feasts upon the trapped unicorn.

The unicorn, serene in nature, was not typically the initiator of chases and fights, whether with lions or humans. Lions were commonly depicted as dancing around, nipping at the unicorn's heels, until out of frustration the unicorn gives chase. Humans, in their hunts of unicorns, were often depicted much like the lion. Always, the goal was to capture the unicorn's healing horn and to tame its wild nature.

CHAPTER 5

Tales of the unicorn's association with primitive people emphasized the unicorn's wildness and untamability. Only primitive humans were able to tame and ride the unicorn. These stories greatly fascinated Charles VI when he became king of France in 1380. As a child, he had fallen to the ground in some kind of seizure and had visions of wild, primitive people riding on the backs of unicorns. Except for the wreaths in their hair, they were completely naked.

Charles VI became obsessed with finding these people so they could lead him to a unicorn. It was all to no avail. During a raucous, costumed celebration that he felt would draw these wild men out, he and six other men were accidentally set on fire. Charles VI was the only survivor. People scoffed when he tried to explain that one of those who perished had been a wild man, drawn out by their celebration. They realized he was no longer fit to govern, and he never found his unicorn.

The unicorn also became known for trying to chase intruders away from its protected environments by frightening or confusing them. A unicorn might raise a frightening noise by clattering its horn against the trees, might vanish and reappear, or lead the pursuers upon an endless, zigzagging chase, wearing out man, horse and hounds.

Although there were a few reported instances of individuals releasing a lion into suspected unicorn habitats, it soon became apparent that not even this method would help capture a unicorn. As a result, newer and more subtle methods of hunting were devised, involving the use of virginal maidens. This has great symbolic significance which will be examined in the chapter on alchemy, but there is no denying the seductive aspect of taming the unicorn. Many pictures and engravings depict a women, often seductive, with her hand upon the horn—a very sexual image—especially for this time in history.

People believed that a virgin presence was necessary for the capture of the unicorn. This virgin was to be placed near a tree in a garden or forest clearing, where the unicorn would be irresistibly drawn to the virgin's purity and childlike beauty. The young maiden would sing softly and the unicorn would draw closer still, then kneel and lay its head upon her lap. The maiden would take a ribbon (in some versions, a golden harness) from her hair and place it over the head of the unicorn. The unicorn would then follow her any where she led it, usually to a holding pen or to a place where the hunters could have at it.

The most commonly recognized version of this tale is depicted in seven embroidered tapestries now hanging in New York's Metropolitan Museum of Art "The Hunt of the Unicorn" shows how a band of hunters track and kill a magnificent white unicorn and bring its body to the castle. In the second tapestry, the unicorn is shown dipping its horn into a stream surrounded by animals. Two of these were a lion and a lioness. In the final tapestry, the unicorn is returned to life.

First Tapestry: The Start of the Hunt

The Metropolitan Museum of Art, Gift of John D. Rockefeller, Jr., The Cloisters Collection, 1937. (37.80.1)

Treasures of the Unicorn

Second Tapestry: The Unicorn Rids the Stream of Poison

The Metropolitan Museum of Art, Gift of John D. Rockefeller, Jr., The Cloisters Collection, 1937. (37.80.2)

Ted Andrews

111

Third Tapestry: The Unicorn Leaps the Stream

The Metropolitan Museum of Art, Gift of John D. Rockefeller, Jr., The Cloisters Collection, 1937. (37.80.3)

TREASURES OF THE UNICORN

Fourth Tapestry: The Unicorn Defends Itself

Ted Andrews

Treasures of the Unicorn

The unicorn is tied to a pomegranate tree, the alchemical prize.

OPPOSITE PAGE

Seventh Tapestry: The Unicorn in Captivity

The Metropolitan Museum of Art, Gift of John D. Rockefeller, Jr., The Cloisters Collection, 1937. (37.80.7)

CHAPTER 5

The Lady and the Unicorn

BENEFITS

• strengthens relationships
• enlarges courage
• enhances trust
• helps overcome
  difficulties and trials
• sharpens discernment
• encourages compatibility

The unicorn teaches us about relationships—with ourselves, with others, with Nature, and with the Divine. If there are difficulties or a lack of clarity in any of these relationships, this magical tale will stimulate new revelations about them, about our role within them, and about our responsibilities. This tale will often teach us which relationships to embrace and which to avoid.

The unicorn is a tireless creature, and so it also teaches us persistence, crucial to success in all areas of life. No matter how talented or gifted a person is, without the ability to persist in endeavors, success will not come. It is not unusual for an individual, after performing this exercise, to have others show up in their lives the following week with solutions to problems, guidance in direction or experience, and assistance with important tasks.

This exercise will reveal our true friends and companions, those who can be trusted. It can reveal the strengths of our friends and invite those into our live whom we can truly depend upon in times of need or trouble.

1. Make all preliminary preparations.

2. Use the Opening and Closing Scenarios described in Chapter 3, Exercise 4 before and after this exercise.

3. Perform the unicorn stance and remember to visualize yourself in the role of one of the characters.

   • If you are having difficulty in your life and need assistance, visualize yourself in the role of the lady to release the energy to manifest help.

   • If you have others who need assistance, visualize yourself in the role of Bartholomew to release the energy to gain insight into the best course of action.

MAGICKAL STORY

THE LADY
AND THE UNICORN

The king of Friesland in the Nether-
lands had a beautiful daughter, Isabel. She was
gifted, smart and adept at falconry. She had
many suitors for her hand in marriage. When
she wed, her father gave her the gift of a unicorn. She
soon became known as the Lady of the Unicorn.

After her marriage, her behavior grew strange. She
was often seen galloping, astride her unicorn, her hair
flowing behind her and her falcon upon her arm. Though
she was married, she continued to entertain suitors. Of
the many who visited her, only one still held her interest.
His name was Bartholomew, and his love for the Lady of
the Unicorn was as great as hers for him, though neither
would attempt to consummate their love because of her
marriage.

Bartholomew was a knight of great adventures. On
one occasion in a distant forest, Bartholomew was
attacked by a great lion whom he tamed and thereafter

rode upon. From that time forth he was known as the Knight of the Lion.[2]

One day, the Lady of the Unicorn was kidnapped and taken to a distant castle, guarded by a dragon. When her husband tried to rescue her, the dragon burned him so seriously that he did not live long after. Many knights followed the husband in death trying to do battle with the dragon. All failed.

Bartholomew heard of the Isabel's kidnapping, mounted his lion and like the husband, went to do battle with the great beast. For days he attempted to get close enough to send a lance through the dragon's belly, but with no success. Every time he got close, the dragon would spew forth vile gas and flames. Both the lion and Bartholomew were singed, but still alive. Again and again he tried. And still he failed.

Just as he was about to try one last time, he saw the lady's unicorn galloping hard down the road toward the dragon. The alicorn glowed, and it ran past the knight and the lion, and lowering its head, it speared the dragon in the belly. It withdrew the horn and prepared to attack again.

The dragon reared and breathed fire and noxious gas, but all rolled off the back of the unicorn with no

---

[2] This character has symbolic ties and connections to esoteric Christianity. Nathaniel, also known as Bartholomew, was one of the 12 apostles, was the one in whom Jesus found no guile. To the early Christian gnostics, Bartholomew was a symbol for the intuition and imagination, representing the dreamers of the world. He embodied the cosmic principles of addition and increase, and he came to also represent those in the astrological sign of Cancer. His primary symbol was the large knife, reflective of the alicorn. It is possible this story arose to reflect further connection between Christ and the unicorn, which will be examined more closely in the next chapter.

effect. The dragon tried to claw the unicorn, but the unicorn was too swift. It dodged and stabbed the dragon again, piercing the dragon through the heart. The dragon fell with a last gasp of flame.

Bartholomew rode quickly, drawing his sword. With a single swipe, he cut off the dragon's head and the dragon turned to ash. The sun burst through the smoke and Bartholomew saw the doors and gates of the castle fly open.

Isabel burst out the front gate and threw her arms around the neck of her unicorn. Her tears of happiness flowed. She then embraced her Knight. Then the Lady of the Unicorn and the Knight of the Lion mounted their magnificent animals and journeyed home together.

CHAPTER 5

EXERCISE 9:   **The Sacred Shield of the Unicorn**

<table>
<tr><td>

BENEFITS

• protection
• balance
• healing
• creation
• virtue and strength

</td></tr>
</table>

Shields have an ancient history. Their creation, decoration, and application are varied, but in most societies the shield was as much practical as it was symbolic. Most people are familiar with the European shields (Coats of Arms) and the medicine shields of the Native Americans. Both served multiple functions, as did the decorated shields in most societies.

In Europe, heraldry became more formalized, but its origins and significance is just as symbolic as in those societies with less formalized traditions. In most societies, heraldry (the creation and decorating of shields) was associated with armorial bearing and originally it served a practical purpose. The flat surfaces lent themselves well to painting, which helped identify opponents in battle.

Many believe that the European heralds were originally minstrels familiar with the various coats of arms, which served an exaggerated function during tournaments and jousts. During medieval times, heraldry develop its own descriptive language and rules. In other parts of the world, it remained less formalized, but just as significant, as with the medicine shield of the native Americans.

> A shield reflected the symbology of a warrior's medicine. "Medicine" to the plains tribes carried a broader scope in its meaning than simple medical healing for physical affliction or injury. Medicine reached into all facets of a person's life. Protection in combat, success in the hunt, success in lovemaking and mate selection, protection from evil doing, and success in visions and dreams were major petitions and were reflected in the symbols found on the Sioux shields.[3]

---

[3] Ed McGaa, Eagle Man, *Mother Earth Spirituality* (San Francisco: Harper, 1990), p. 158.

The Lion and the Unicorn

As in heraldry, the medicine shields could be simple or intricate. They could represent family, tribe or the individual. Unlike the shields of Europe, the medicine shields were usually circular. They represented the never-ending cycle of life, death and rebirth—no beginning and no end. It reflects the Medicine Wheel, the Sacred Loop—the symbol of all of life's cycles.

TYPICAL EUROPEAN HERALDIC SHIELD

Real and mythical animals significant to the individual would often appear as totems. The shield bearer established a relationship with totems by becoming familiar with the animal's unique characteristics, and the animal totem could also be a special spirit helper to the individual. An animal's picture on the shield became a way of invoking its energy.

Shields could show recurring dreams or visions. Colors reflecting specific qualities were used in their creation. An individual's special gifts or uniqueness could appear on a shield in a symbolic manner. Shields are ceremonial, religious, spiritual, and armorial. There are shields for countries, counties, towns, cities, and families. Shields represent different aspects of life or can encompasses all of life.

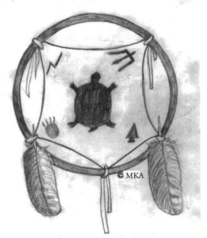

Native American Medicine Shield Design

There is no limit to the number or types of shields we can have. We can create a shield for protection or a shield for healing, a spirit shield for our work with other realms and dimensions, or a personal shield reflecting all aspects of ourselves, spiritual and physical.

CHAPTER 5

Two things should be kept in mind throughout that construction of any shield:

- The shield speaks of who you are.
- All things deliberately made accurately reflect those who make them and the forces represented

Although some societies had formalized rules for making shields, it is not necessary to follow rigid formulas. Shields can be made from any material, constructed from metal or cloth, drawn upon paper or painted on a wall. They can be whatever shape we believe is most significant for its purpose.

Whether we actually construct a shield or simply sketch or paint one, the process is powerful. On one level it becomes a talisman, yantra, or mandala. Mandalas and yantras are geometric designs created to express and invoke specific archetypal energies in the physical or the spiritual realms. They awaken a sense of our relationship to ourselves and to the forces of the universe, providing bridges to archetypal forces, linking the physical and spiritual dimensions.

Mandalas hold the essence of a thought or a concept, and are designed to draw our consciousness more fully into that concept. They stimulate our inner creative forces in a manner peculiar to their design.

TRADITIONAL HERALDIC VOCABULARY	
BLAZON	the language used to describe shields of arms, crests & badges
DEXTER	the left side of the shield (as it is faced)
SINISTER	the right side of the shield (as it is faced)
FIELD	the surface of the shield
PER PALE	shield field that is divided vertically
PER FESS	shield field that is divided horizontally
PER BEND	shield field that is divided diagonally
PER CROSS	shield field divided into quarters
PER SALTIRE	shield field with multiple lines (diagonal)
ORDINARIES	principle shapes
CHARGES	significant animals, mythical beasts or inanimate objects. The animals were usually in one of four positions:

1. **rampant**: standing on one hind leg
2. **passant**: walking past
3. **displayed**: outstretched wings
4. **sejant**: seated erect

Shields, like mandalas, can be constructed to arouse any inner force we desire. They become tools for integration and transformation, action and interaction with ourselves and our life.

When you create your own shield with a unicorn, several things will automatically occur. You will find yourself and your relationship to the unicorn strengthened and the unicorn's energy activated. The shield be-

TRADITIONAL HERALDIC CHARGES	
ANCHOR	= faith
APPLE	= good luck
ARM	= power
ARROW	= authority
AXE	= strength
BEAR	= defender
BEE	= industrious
BOAT	= venture
BULL	= protecto
BOAR	= perseverance
CRANE	= vigilance
CROSS	= dedication
CROWN	= royalty
DOG	= fidelity
DOVE	= faith
EAGLE	= superiority
HEART	= gentleness
HORSE	= speed
KEY	= knowledge
KNIFE	= sacrifice
LION	= strength
MACE	= authority
PELICAN	= sacrifice and faith
SERPENT	= defiance
STAG	= purity
TOWER	= defense
UNICORN	= virtue
DRAGON	= knowledge & power

TRADITIONAL HERALDIC COLORS		
GULES	=	red (fire and fortitude)
OR	=	gold (purity and valor)
AZURE	=	blue (loyalty and truth)
ARGENT	=	white (peace and nobility)
VERT	=	green (strength and freshness)
PURPURE	=	purple (justice, majesty, royalty)
SABLE	=	black (royalty and repentence)
ERMINE	=	black tails on white (valor and leadeship)
VAIR	=	pattern of blue and white (truth and purity)

comes a mirror, reflecting the unicorn into your life more dynamically. When the lion is combined with the unicorn on a shield, balance and harmony begin to manifest during the construction process. Aggravations begin to disappear and things which have not been working begin to work once more. Flow and balance begin to be restored.

CHAPTER 5

NATIVE AMERICAN & SHAMANIC SHIELD SYMBOLS
(DIRECTIONS)

Seneca Tradition

EAST	air; mind; creativity; yellow
SOUTH	fire; inspiration; purification; red
WEST	water; emotion; intuition; blue
NORTH	earth; body; prosperity; green

Sioux Tradition

EAST	wind; wolf; red hawk; red
SOUTH	fire; buffalo; bear; yellow
WEST	water; thunderbird; black horse; black
NORTH	earth; eagle; snowy owl; white

Chippewa Tradition

EAST	spring; eagle; red and gold
SOUTH	summer; coyote; green and yellow
WEST	autumn; grizzly bear; deep blues and black
NORTH	winter; white buffalo; white

SHAPES AND THEIR SIGNIFICANCE

circle	= wholeness, complete, circle of life, calmness
square	= balance, solidness, the four elements, stability
triangle	= power, amplification, energizing, strengthening
diamond	= creativity, activation, stimulating
crescent	= feminine, creative intuition, emotional calm
cross	= balance of elements, harmonizing polarities or opposites
six-rayed star	= healing, strengthening and protecting

Simple ideas for creating your own unicorn shield follow.

- Do not limit your creation to these ideas.
- Study heraldry. It will provide some wonderful inspiration.
- Follow your own heart and design. That is what the unicorn teaches, especially in using our creative energies. You will find as you create additional shields, they will grow in power and significance.

Different native peoples had their own correspondences in colors and animals. These were used in making the medicine shields. If you have ancestors linked to a particular tribe, you may find it more beneficial to study their correspondences. If you are drawn to a particular tradition, study it as well. Remember that the more significance you can incorporate into your shield, the greater the power your shield will have.

Making Your Sacred Unicorn Shield

The making of the shield itself is a sacred process, and the more thought and focus you put into it, the greater its power. Everything that you put on your shield will have significance. It is good to know why you use the colors you choose.

Honor That Feeling!

The unicorn teaches trust, and the color may be what is best for you at the time of construction. Although you may initially decide on a predominant color, once you get started, you may find that it doesn't quite suit you.

Keep in mind also that the shield may change in the construction process. The creation of the shield is never truly completed. Over several months or even years, you may add new images, variations, and colors to your shield, reflecting your growth and new depths you are achieving.

I have several shield designs I created years ago that I still add to periodically. My totem animal shield contains a multitude of animals added to over the years, animals including my power totems as well as other animals that have appeared in my life at significant times and for special purposes.

Additions to spiritual shields are natural. They reflect changes in spiritual growth and perception. As your spiritual depths expand, add new symbols and variations. Change is part of life and reflects an increasing variety of significant forces you have learned or are learning to draw upon and use within your day-to-day life.

CHAPTER 5

Initially, you will want to draw or sketch your shield prior to actually constructing one. Even the simple act of drawing will actualize the associated energies associated. Anytime we do something physical like this, we are drawing those forces out of that vague ethereal realm and setting them into motion more dynamically within our physical life.

Concentration in the creating of the shield is important. Prior to actually starting, you may wish to meditate upon it, and once you start, make sure you will be undisturbed while working. The creation of the shield is an active meditation in itself. You are activating the right brain, programming it to respond to the images, symbols, and significance of the shield and all of its reflective energies.

1. Begin by gathering together your materials. You will need drawing utensils, paper, scissors, and coloring media.

    •   If you cannot draw (or feel that you can't), obtain pictures of the unicorn that you can trace or cut out. Do the same thing with the lion. Since this shield is for balance, we will use both.

    •   If you intend to only draw the shield rather than actually make one, you will want to draw it the size of poster board so it will be easier to hang and focus upon in meditation.

2. Determine the colors. Choose your favorites or those you find calming.

    •   You may even want to use opposite colors, as they balance each other: red and green, black and white, orange and blue, purple and gold.

    •   Learn something about the hidden significance of the colors you choose. Most colors are symbolic and a study of your choices may reveal much about yourself and the energies you will be invoking through this shield.

3. Decide on a basic shape for your shield. It may be a typical heraldic form or any other shape.

   - The more significance we attach to the shape, the greater the effect. Geometric shapes affect electromagnetic patterns, stimulating and eliciting definable effects.

   - If unsure of a shape, I suggest using a circular or square field. These are effective for every type of shield that you might wish to create.

4. Take your drawing paper or your poster board and create the basic shield form (circle, square, or whatever you have chosen) in the center. Leave enough space around the edges so you will be able to add images and symbols.

   - Some people like to place the unicorn and lion inside the circle, while others like to do so outside. For some, the inner placement symbolizes the animals' energies alive and active within them. For others, the outer placement reflects their guardianship and protection of the life environment.

   - One is no better than the other. Whichever you choose, know why. This adds power to the creation process and to its ultimate effectiveness.

   - For our purposes, I recommend that the unicorn be placed on one side of the shield and the lion upon the opposite. This reflects balance, which is part of this shield's purpose.

5. Place the colors and other symbols in this shield which are significant to your life and to the purpose of this shield.

   - Since this shield is for protection and balance, ask yourself, "What other symbols and images do I associate with balance, health, and protection?"

   - Arranging symbols upon the shield is a creative process. Place them in whatever manner you think best for you. Just make sure that you know the purpose and significance of each.

   - Use the colors, like symbols, in the manner best for you. Place colors in different sections as you feel appropriate.

6. Place something personal in a central position upon the shield. This is something that represents you, activating the shield's energies to flow into the center of your life.

7. When you finish the drawing or construction, set it across the floor from you and just gaze softly upon it and all of its elements for ten to fifteen minutes. Feel its energies.

   • Review in your mind its many significances. Visualize it working for you. See events changing, harmonizing, and balancing.

   • Know that by its construction you have released the energy of balance into your physical life.

   • Avoid being critical of the shield. The idea is not to demonstrate artistic abilities, but to tap into archetypal energies and to draw them out and manifest them more dynamically. Early shamans and primitive peoples are not considered artistically gifted, but their shields and drawings were imbued with a significance and power that was very primal.

   • As you imbue the making of the shield and all of its elements with significance, it will attain its own beauty and primal power.

8. Over the next several days or even a week, you may feel that some changes are necessary. Follow through on them. When you are satisfied, you may wish to hang the drawing where you can see it everyday, or you may wish to construct an actual shield. This can be done with cloth, wood, metal or any of a variety of ways, depending upon how much time and effort you wish to put into it.

9. Feel free to add to your shield from time to time. Create new ones.

    •   If you reach a point where you are not sure what to add, just stop. You have probably created one that is suitable for you at the moment. Trust that it will evolve and change as you do. Shields will take on a life of their own as you construct or draw them. This is good! It's a positive sign that the shield is already working.

    •   You may find in the process of creating a shield that you lose track of time. This is also a positive sign that you have touched and activated those archetypal energies associated with the symbols of the shield. You have been drawn into its energy.

EXERCISE 10: # The Hunt of the Unicorn

BENEFITS
• compassion
• clarity of direction
• stamina
• trust
• spiritual direction
• discernment of who and what to trust

One of the most famous tales of the unicorn was depicted upon the tapestries described earlier in this chapter. As with most tales of the unicorn, there is great hidden significance. To some this tale is one of betrayal. To others, one of redemption. It embodies the stamina of the unicorn and its ability to be reborn, even after being captured.

The yearning for the unicorn and its magnificent properties was often great. The hunt would take precedence over everything else, becoming the all. Everything but the capture would be lost in this passion. If nothing else, this tale is reminds us there is responsibility in all acts, that in the pursuit of our dreams, we must not lose sight of ourselves. The sacred quest for the Holy Grail in is the gift—not finding the grail itself. It is life's journey which holds our greatest treasures—not its end.

This tale teaches us to follow our heart and our spirit, that if we are true to our heart, we can still succeed. It reminds us that there is a true way to pursue our dreams and there is a false way. It teaches that the false way has consequences that bring the death of dreams and the loss of heart, that the promise of reward at the expense of the innocent is an empty promise; both the dream and the dreamer will be lost.

Magickal storytelling with this particular tale had a surprising effect the first time I tried it. Within a week, I received multiple confirmations as to whom I could trust and whom I couldn't. It was a very illuminating week, and in many respects very sad. I discovered friends who really weren't friends and business relationships that were dishonest and deceptive. Although hesitant to believe such things at first, events played out quickly and repeatedly to remove any doubts whatsoever! Since that first magical storytelling with this tale, the results every time have been the same. Within a week, I discovered dishonest practices and deceptions. I also discovered those whose trust is true, strong, and reliable. This occurs with most people who perform this exercise.

Although a variety of the benefits listed may unfold, the trust issues seem to surface most strongly and clearly of them all. Therefore, a word of caution is advised.

CAUTION!

If you are not sure you wish to uncover the truth about others in your life or about your own trustworthiness (and some people prefer to remain blind to deceptions around them), DO NOT USE THIS EXERCISE.

Perform this magickal storytelling in the same manner as the others, preparing for it and grounding the energy afterwards as described in Chapter 3, Exercise 4. Make the necessary preparation. Use the same introduction and conclusion. Use the magical unicorn stance as described earlier.

Try this exercise in two ways:

- See yourself as the unicorn, and

- See yourself as the young maiden who mourns the loss of the unicorn and following her heart, leaves the castle. Then pay close attention to the events that unfold over the following week. If you have ever been unsure of how meditation elicits tangible effects within your day-to-day life, this exercise will make it clear.

MAGICKAL STORY:

THE HUNT OF THE UNICORN

The nobles would often gather at dawn on the day of the hunt. On days when the hunt would be for the unicorn, a crowd gathered with them. Some were families of the hunters, excited over the possibility of such a wondrous prize as the unicorn. Others were there to protest. To them, the unicorn was forbidden fruit. They believed that hunting it was a transgression against God and all that was divine. Their protests always fell upon deaf ears.

The horses shifted nervously and the dogs seemed more excited than usual. They pulled on their leads and bayed. They snipped at the heels of each other. Today was a special hunt. They could feel it. There was something in the air. Although the unicorn hunts had been unsuccessful in the past, everyone seemed to sense that today would be a great adventure. Today would bring the success they desired.

The houndsmen and their dogs went ahead of the hunters, the dogs' noses sniffing the air for that spiced, exotic scent. Their warm breath was visible in the cool morning air. They were anxious to run. They were anx-

ious for the pursuit. Their primal instincts were awake and sharper than usual.

Then the lead hound caught the scent of cinnamon and spice. It bayed once and then jumped at the lead. The dogs barked and danced, pulling at their leads. The houndsmen turned the dogs loose and they dashed toward the distant woods. They bounded through the thicket, the scent strong within their nose. The hunters followed, their horses spurred.

The unicorn stood by a stream. Its silver hooves caught the early morning sunlight. Its eyes were a soft blue-gray. The horn stood proud. Its spiral markings made the pearlescence seem alive. The unicorn paused only long enough to touch the horn to the stream. The water bubbled and rippled, purified, and its surface became like liquid diamonds.

Then the unicorn jumped, quickly outdistancing the hounds. The hunters paused as they watched the wonder of this creature. The beauty touched them and for a moment they lost the desire of pursuit. Then a houndsman blew the horn and the moment was shattered. Hounds and hunters appeared from all sides at the sound of the horn. The unicorn stood still, its sharp eyes watching the hunters encircle it. As the hunters caught sight of the unicorn, some held back. It was too beautiful. The sun glinted off the silver mane and the alicorn shimmered with light.

From the back of the hunters, a spear flew through the air, as one gave into the desire for blood. The spear's sharp edge cut into the flank of the unicorn and the red blood stood out brightly against its milk white coat. Its

eyes flashed, but not a sound was uttered. It jumped and lowered its head, charging the nearest hunters. Their horses dodged to the side to avoid being gored by the horn. The movement created a gap in the hunters' midst and the unicorn dashed through it. As the hunters and hounds turned to pursue, no one noticed that where the unicorn's blood had touched the ground, roses had sprung up from the earth.

The unicorn looked back, surprised to still see the hunters in such pursuit. The wound to the flank was slowing the unicorn, and soon the hounds were nipping at its legs. The unicorn's breathing was rapid and its heart pounded. The sounds of the hunters and their hounds were grating and unnerving, but the unicorn's heart pounded stronger.

The unicorn reared, bringing itself to an abrupt stop. It kicked with its powerful rear legs and a hound was sent flying, silenced. The unicorn lowered its head and gored another hound. Squeals of pain caused the other hounds to pull up. Now more wary and cautious, they circled the unicorn. Their eyes shone with fire. There was no feeling in the hounds. Only blood lust.

The heavy breathing of the unicorn grew louder. A wind arose in response, sending a spiral of dust around the unicorn, blinding the dogs. The unicorn used the opportunity to make its escape yet again.

Covered with sweat, the unicorn again outdistanced the hunters and hounds, leaving them behind. Covered with sweat and dried blood upon its wounded flank, the

unicorn circled back toward the castle. The sounds of the hunters and their hounds faded in the distance.

As the unicorn moved silently around the castle, it spied a fenced rose garden where three women sat, two older and one younger. Their voices were soft and gentle and sounded to the unicorn's ears like tinkling bells. Sad and wounded from the chase, the unicorn felt this was a safe place to rest.

The women exclaimed softly as the unicorn approached. The one nearest him, the youngest one, had eyes that were sad, but she reached out her slim hand and softly stroked the unicorn's muzzle. Looking at her, the unicorn saw her eyes were filled with tears. To comfort her, the unicorn rubbed its neck against the arm of the young maiden. At that moment, the unicorn caught a movement out of the corner of its eye. One of the other women was waving her hand in the air.

The unicorn knew he should run, but the touch of the young maiden seemed innocent enough. Before it could move, hounds and hunters appeared from all corners of the garden. The dogs snarled and growled. A hunter stepped forward and thrust his spear into the unicorn's side. The unicorn looked at the spear, which felt like lightning piercing its side, and then upon the faces of the three women, particularly the young maiden who had stroked him. Her face was buried in her hands.

Tricked! Trapped! And now wounded!

Then another spear struck. And another. The hounds leaped upon the unicorn, biting and tearing at its white

flesh. Before long there was no sign of white. Only red—blood red.

The unicorn died neither quickly nor easily. But it did die. The body became less luminous. The silver mane and hooves lost their shimmer, and the horn turned yellow and mottled.

And then the alicorn was cut from the head.

The hunters and the people of the castle cheered loudly and began to celebrate. They danced about the castle and through its great halls. The three women stood alone in the garden. The one who had stroked the unicorn was the most distraught. The older two explained that it was their duty to lure the unicorn into a false sense of security. It was the only way to capture it. It would have been killed anyway, they rationalized. The young maiden just turned away from them. She felt her heart dying.

Then the one who signaled the hunters looked about the garden to find the hunters and hounds had trampled all of the beautiful rose bushes. Only one remained, and only one rose was left upon it. She picked that single red rose from the surviving bush and gave it to the distraught maiden, hoping to console her.

The young maiden held the rose limp and loose within her hand. It did not help. It did nothing to console her. She sat down upon a garden bench and stared blankly at the rose in her hand. Like her, it seemed to no longer have life. The two older women frowned at such naivete' and then turned to join the celebration as the songs and shouts from inside the castle carried out into the garden. The young maiden was left alone.

The young maiden shuddered over the celebration of such a cruel act. She knew she could never look upon these people the same ever again. She doubted that she could live here any longer. She stood and walked from the castle grounds still holding the red rose. She walked toward the distant woods and then sat herself down at the edge of a stream—the very stream the unicorn had purified before the chase began. She began to weep over what she had done.

As the sun set, her crying began to cease. She washed her face in the cool water and looked at the rose she had been given. In the time she had been at this stream, it had already wilted. She tossed it into the stream and watched as the stream carried it away from her to a bend not far away. There it became tangled and hung upon other stream debris. She watched the waters wash over the rose and began to weep once more.

As the moon rose and grew bright overhead, she could see her distorted reflection upon the surface of the stream. Then, from the corner of her eye, she caught a glint. As she looked down the stream, she saw a flash of white by what was left of her flower. A breeze carried to her the faint scent of cinnamon and apple blossom, and she stood. Her eyes looked about, and she moved slowly to where her wilted rose had hung up in the stream.

Her eyes widened. She stared at the flower in the stream. She reached down to draw it from the water, her heart pounding. No longer was it wilted! No longer was it red! Now it was the most beautiful white rose she had ever seen!

Ted Andrews

As she drew it out of the stream, she heard a soft tinkling of bells. She raised her head and caught the white flash of the unicorn as it disappeared into the woods and the night. She held the flower close to her as her heart began to fill with hope once more.

Notes

CHAPTER 6

The Unicorn and Christ

It has in the middle of its brow a single horn...they lead forth a young virgin, pure and chaste, to whom, when the animal sees her, he approaches...Then the girl, while sitting quietly, reaches forth her hand and grasps the horn on the animal's brow, and at this point the huntsmen come up and take the beast...Likewise the Lord Christ has raised up for us a horn of salvation in the midst of Jerusalem, in the house of God, by the intercession of the mother of God, a virgin pure, chaste, full of mercy, immaculate, inviolate.

Anecdota Syriaca,
J.P.N. Land, trans.
p. 146

The Unicorn of Christ

In the 3rd century BC, an event would occur that in the next fifteen hundred years would be a dominant influence in spreading the belief in unicorns throughout Europe. The first seven books of the Bible was translated by 72 Alexandrian Jewish scholars from the Hebrew to the Greek. This translation came to be known as the *Septuagint*.

Although the scholars did not know much about the *re'em*, an animal involved in this translation, they knew was it was large, fierce, and horned. In the translation, the re'em would become *monoceros*, which would eventually be Latinized into *unicornis*. The unicorn officially entered Biblical lore here.

Although only references are found to the unicorn in the Bible, actual tales of it are found in the Talmud and in Jewish folklore. In Talmudic lore, there are tales of the unicorn with Noah, Job, and the prophets Daniel and David. In one tale, the uni-

> *When God created the earth, he made a river which flowed from the Garden of Eden... Then God told Adam to name the animals... and the first animal he named was the unicorn. When the Lord heard the name that Adam had spoken, he reached down and touched the tip of the single horn growing from the animal's forehead. From that moment on, the unicorn was elevated above other beasts.*
>
> Nancy Hathaway
> *The Unicorn*[1]
> pp. 29-30

corn is the first animal named by Adam and thus considered sacred by God. (See quote in box.) In this tale, upon Adam's and Eve's expulsion from the Garden of Eden, the unicorn was given a choice to stay in paradise or leave with them and enter the world of pain and suffering. The unicorn watched Adam and Eve, and then followed after them, a symbol of hope and strength. For this act of compassion, the unicorn was forever blessed.

There exist several versions of the story of Noah and the unicorn. Probably the most common one I heard as a child in catechism class. A

---

[1] Nancy Hathaway, *The Unicorn* (New York: Viking Press, 1980), pp. 29-30. From The *Unicorn* by Nancy Hathaway. Copyright ©1980 by Nancy Hathaway and Rosebud Books, Inc. Used by permission of Viking Penguin, a division of Penguin Books USA, Inc.

tiny old nun, a marvelous storyteller, related in her version, how the unicorn, being the strongest of all the animals, chose to swim rather than ride within the ark. Over the many months after the deluge, Noah would send out birds to find dry land. The unicorn, with its keen eyesight, always saw the birds go out and would follow their flight. When no land was found, the birds would tire and not enough strength to return to the ark. The birds would see unicorn's head and horn in the water below and land upon it to rest. Noah sent many birds out and they piled high upon the unicorn's head and horn, weighing down even the strong unicorn and eventually drowning it.

For many, these tales explained the once visible presence of unicorns in the world. For others, the tales amplified the mysticism surrounding the animal and awakened a spiritual fascination for it. One such tale centers around Daniel, a prophet from the Old Testament. Daniel was a dreamer and dream interpreter, the soothsayer for King Nebuchadnezzar. At night, his dreams were visionary. From them he gained great secrets and could tell the future. In one of these visionary dreams, Daniel first encountered the unicorn. It is partly from this tale and others like it that the unicorn became a symbol for the protector of dreams and dreamers.

In this dream, Daniel saw a ram standing near the bank of the river Ulai. It had two horns, one larger than the other. With each breath, the ram grew stronger, more warlike and fierce. Before long it was invincible. Then a unicorn appeared with its magnificent single horn. It lowered its head and horn and stalked toward the ram. With every step, the water in the river rippled and broke against the banks with the force of a tidal wave. As the ram began to charge, the unicorn severed the rams horns with its own single horn and knocked the beast into the river. Upon trampling the ram into the depths of the water, the unicorn began to grow to the heights of heaven. Its horn, now tipped with blood, broke off and out from it sprang four other horns.

At the time, the meaning was lost to Daniel. While searching for the meaning, the angel Gabriel appeared to Daniel and told him of the dream's significance: the ram's horns were the kings of Medea and Persia. The unicorn's horn was Alexander, who would conquer the land. When Alexander died, four kings would rise up to divide Alexander's territory. Daniel related this information to Nebuchadnezzar, and eventually the events played out in history.

To many, this tale reflects great changes in history. To astrologers, though, it is a signal to the end of the Arien age and the beginning of the Piscean. To still others, this dream is the first link between the unicorn and the one the world would come to know as Jesus Christ. The ram symbolized not only Rome as it rose to great power, but also all other religions that would fall to the teachings of Christ. The connection between Jesus and the unicorn was foreshadowed in the Old Testament.

Within the New Testament, the genealogy of Jesus fulfilled the messianic prophecies found in the Old Testament, particularly in the Book of Isaiah, which indicated the messiah would be a descendent of King David. The Gospel of Matthew (1:17) says, "So all generations from Abraham to David were fourteen generations, and from David to Babylon fourteen generations, and the deportation to Babylon to the Christ fourteen generations." This suggests that the messiah would come through a descendent of the Diaspora Jews, those forced to scatter from

---

SEVEN UNICORN REFERENCES IN THE BIBLE

God brought them out of Egypt; he hath as it were the strength of the unicorn.

Numbers 23, 22

His glory is like the firstling of his bullock, and his hors are like the horns of the unicorn: with them he shall push the people together to the ends of the earth.

Deuteronomy 23, 17

Save me from the lion's mouth; for thou hast heard me from the horns of the unicorns.

Psalm 22, 21

He maketh them also to skip like a calf; Lebanon and Sirion like a young unicorn.

Psalm 26, 6

But my horn shalt thou exalt like the horn of the unicorn: I shall be anointed with fresh oil.

Psalm 92, 10

And the unicorn shall come down with them, and the bullocks with their bulls; and their land shall be soaked with blood, and their dust made fat with fatness.

Isaiah 34, 7

Will the unicorn be willing to serve thee or abide in thy crib? Canst thou bind the unicorn with his band in the furrow? Or will he harrow the valleys after thee? Wilt thou trust him because his strength is great? Or will thou leave thy labour to him? Wilt thou believe him, that he will bring home thy seed, and gather it into thy barn?

Job 39, 9-12

CHAPTER 6

around Babylon. David experienced the unicorn first hand, but for Jesus, the descendent of David, the unicorn would become a symbol.

The psalmist David was the youngest of eight sons. As he tended the family's sheep, he wandered the hills and valleys, learning their secrets and creating songs upon his harp. Often mocked and picked upon by his brothers, he felt the family had laid responsibilities upon him that were unjust. On one such occasion, to forget his anger, he decided to explore a distant mountain. As David climbed, he felt a ringing in the air about him and every cell in his body seemed to buzz with new life. A magnificent sound arose from every direction, the sound of the name of God, and his body vibrated in tune with it.

David felt movement beneath his feet, a rumbling and trembling like an earthquake. Still he continued to climb, and the mountain's movements became more animated. It was then he realized this was not a mountain, but the back of a great unicorn! He climbed on, holding onto the flowing mane. Before long he saw the horn. It was of gold and ivory and it shined brighter than the sun.

As David stood upon the head of the unicorn, the Lord sent down from the heavens a great lion. The beast fixed its eyes upon David, and David began to tremble with fear. When the unicorn, fearing no other animal, knelt on the ground in respect to this lion, David was sure he was about to die. David slid from the back of the unicorn and crouched in fear as the lion approached. As the lion drew near, the sounds in the air grew louder and stronger, and David was stirred in his heart to sing this song:

> Be not thou far from me, O Lord:
> Deliver my soul from the sword;
> My darling from the power of the dog.
> Save me from the lion's mouth;
> For thou hast heard me from the horns of the unicorns.
>
> (Psalms 22: 20-22)

The Unicorn of Christ

The lion heard David's song, and it paused a moment before approaching more slowly. The fierce beast soon stood before David, watching the young man tremble as he continued to sing this song. In amazement, David saw the lion kneel at his feet.

Although the Jewish tales are not contained in the Bible itself, there are still seven distinct Old Testament references to it. Two references to the unicorn are found in the Pentateuch, one in the Book of Job, one in the Book of Isaiah, and three in the Book of Psalms.

With the eventual spread of Christianity throughout Europe, the seven Old Testament references to this animal in the King James version of the Bible familiarized the Middle Ages general public with the unicorn. The unicorn lost most of its Jewish overtones and became a frequent Christian symbol as its spiritual associations grew stronger and more powerful in the minds of the people. Even as early as 4th century, associations between Jesus Christ and the unicorn began to surface in the Church:

> Who is the unicorn but the only begotten Son of God...Christ is the Power—therefore he is called the unicorn on the ground that he has one horn, that is, one common power with the father. (Saint Ambrose, Bishop of Milan)[2]

Church leaders saw in the unicorn tale the continuing battle between Christ and Satan. The tale of serpents loosing venom into streams at night and the unicorn's purification of the stream with its alicorn are well known. The serpent was a common image for Satan. The healing powers of Christ were likened to the unicorn's. Leaders of the Church desired and searched for unicorn horns, likening them to the Holy Grail. Drinking from unicorn horns would heal the soul and cleanse the spirit.

The unicorn became a common symbol for the Church, was engraved upon altars, depicted on tapestries, and its image used in sermons and

---

[2] Nancy Hathaway, *The Unicorn* (New York: Viking Press, 1980), p. 14. From The *Unicorn* by Nancy Hathaway. Copyright ©1980 by Nancy Hathaway and Rosebud Books, Inc. Used by permission of Viking Penguin, a division of Penguin Books USA, Inc.

CHAPTER 6

MADONNA AND UNICORN

*In paintings such as this, the link between the unicorn and Christ was
made very explicit and frequently found within the art of the Middle Ages.*

"Madonna and Unicorn" by Spanish Forger. Pierpont Morgan Library, New York. M786A, f.64.

moral teachings. During this time, the association of the unicorn with the virgin grew tremendously, a captured unicorn, head upon the lap of a young virginal maiden, a common depiction. For many, this scene was reminiscent of images of the Christ child and the Madonna, and so there arose not only the correspondence of the unicorn and Christ, but also a correspondence between the virgin and the mother of Jesus.

The commonly held notion that a virgin was required to capture a unicorn did not originate with the Church. Physiologus, a naturalist from the 5th century AD, compiled a bestiary, *The Physiologus*. He describes the unicorn as a small but fierce animal that could only be captured by a virgin. The virgin's purity as well as her scent attracted the unicorn, which would then lay its head upon the virgin's lap.

The Church employed the virgin image throughout the Middle Ages to teach morality. The notion that without chastity, Christians could not know Christ became a means to motivate the lay people toward sexual purity and even a monastic life, yet strong sexual undertones remained with the unicorn image. The connotations of a virgin capture of the unicorn had implicit erotic aspects that would also show up in medieval art.

Questions arose as to whether the unicorn could be captured by true virgins or pretend virgins—whether purity and chastity were of the heart or of the body. The mystic Hildegarde de Bingen wrote that the virgins should not be mere rustics, but had to be well born.[3] Statements and teachings such as these reveal much about how the Church would mislead and misuse the unicorn image for its own benefit.

The Church was not always a good source of information, as its interpretation of the unicorn often varied and conflicted. At times, the unicorn was a symbol of chastity for women and of valor and nobility for men. At other times it represented solitude and the monastic life, and even illicit sexuality and sodomy. It was used to symbolize earthly and heavenly love, but also death and violence. A 15th century painting by Albrecht Durer (1471-1528), *The Rape of Persephone*, depicts Pluto carrying off

---

[3] Hildegarde de Bingen, "viii, 5," *Physica*.

THE ANNUNCIATION

*To the Church, the unicorn was a symbol of chastity, but even Church
leaders could not agree on this. Though depicted with the Madonna,
the unicorn was also depicted with other women, also virginal
but very seductive. The capture of the unicorn by a virgin
always had erotic connotations.*

"The Annunciation" by Spanish Forger. Pierpont Morgan Library, New York. G.5, f.18v.

Persephone on a unicorn. In this case, the unicorn symbolizes death and destruction.

The unicorn horn, though phallic, was also a symbol of the sexual power in control. To the Christian mystics at the time, it was a symbol of the spear which pierced the side of Christ upon the cross, and also the cup that captured the blood from the wound, the source of many grail legends.

In spite of the often contradictory interpretations, Medieval Christian mystics regularly employed the unicorn as a symbol for Christ, epitomizing the spiritual life of humanity. The single horn represented what we call today the brow chakra or third eye area of the body, linked to the part of the brain serving as our spiritual vision center. The unicorn came to represent the illumined spiritual nature. Many believe that the horn of salvation, mentioned by St. Luke in Biblical scripture, is the horn of the unicorn. It alone pricks the hearts of humans, turning toward consideration of salvation through Christ.

If nothing else, the association of the unicorn with the Christ figure reveals the archetypal power of this image, with ties to energies beyond the mere physical, beyond any one religion, a link to the divine archetypal energies running through all religions and all traditions.

CHAPTER 6

The Holy Quest

BENEFITS
• clarity of life purpose
• stimulation of new opportunities
• prosperity on own path
• new choices of renewed spirituality

The Holy Quest is the quest for our spiritual purpose and how best to express it within our life. It has been called by many names throughout the ages, although the Quest for the Holy Grail is the most common. To many, the grail cup is simply the cup that caught the blood of Jesus while on the cross, but it has meanings and significance much older and deeper.

All cups, bowls, and cauldrons are archetypal symbols of the feminine forces. They reflect the energy of the womb from which new life may be born, the unmanifest with all of its possibilities, the primal feminine wisdom, illumination, and intuition: "The feminine, in its symbol of the bowl (or cup), reflects itself through mystery. It is a gate through which we may enter or leave."[4]

The cup is also tied to the energies of the cornucopia. The unicorn's spiral horn, cone shaped, most resembles the cornucopia or the *horn of plenty*. The cornucopia, from the horn of Amaltheia, became the constellation for Capricorn (the unicorn has often been depicted in a goat form). A symbol of infinite supply, the cornucopia reminds us we can use its image to multiply what we have within our lives, teaching us that giving never diminishes our own supplies or energies.

The Holy Quest is one which brings us into touch with our true self and opens the doors to pursuing its expression within our daily lives. It serves two distinct purposes:

• the search to discover and awaken our true spiritual essence, our innermost self, and

• the quest for our spiritual path in this lifetime, the best way to express that true essence during this incarnation.

---

[4] Ted Andrews, *Crystal Balls & Crystal Bowls* (St. Paul: Llewellyn Publications, 1995), p. 129.

Please note, the spiritual quest is not a quest that leads into a light in which all of our troubles are dissolved. It is a quest to find that light and manifest it within out day-to-day circumstances.

The form of the quest takes many shapes. For some it may result in becoming a teacher or worker in the metaphysical or spiritual field. For others, it may take the form of simply living the daily life in a creative, productive manner. The ultimate form of the quest is not the most important factor, but rather that we pursue some Holy Quest. Regardless of the form of the quest, all who go forth and follow through upon it will achieve their aim.

In many traditions, the unicorn was depicted as related to the deer, considered the most important animal ever hunted. The deer hunt moves us from the civilization path back to the primal wilderness. Many tales and myths speak of deer luring hunters deep into the woods where they become lost and then encounter a variety of new adventures which renew and reshape them. These adventures involve encounters with new people and situations which provide opportunities to capture the grail or to find a new path to it.

In many of these tales, there is an encounter with one who serves as a guide and teacher. In this exercise, this role is filled by Auriel, the angel of alchemy and vision. Auriel oversees the work of all nature spirits, helping humanity awaken to them. An angelic being, Auriel helps open our vision of the Faerie Realm more fully and consciously, a great being who can assist us in experiencing an actual encounter with the unicorn.

The colors of Auriel vary from tradition to tradition. Usually, when the contact occurs with some aspect of the Faerie Realm, Auriel will appear in the colors of yellow and black or in just white. Auriel shares the symbol of the flaming sword with the archangel Michael. In Grail legends, the sword was interchangeable with the spear or lance that pierced the side of Jesus upon the cross.

This exercise will stimulate a lot of changes or opportunities for change in daily life, usually making themselves evident within three days.

CHAPTER 6

New offers or opportunities may present themselves; new ideas for creative projects may surface, new opportunities to move or to leave one position to start another may arise. This exercise reveals the promise of opportunities—spiritual and physical—part of what the unicorn leads us to. Remember, though, that although the opportunities may arise, it is still your choice whether to act or not, your decision to determine if these opportunities will benefit you.

Begin this exercise in the same way you have done with the others. Make your preparations. Perform the unicorn stance (See Chapter 3, Exercise 4). Then make yourself comfortable, and as you relax, allow the opening scenario to unfold within the mind. Visualize, imagine, and feel each, knowing that as you focus upon them, they will elicit discernible results within your daily life!

THE HOLY QUEST

Your are seated beneath the apple tree, next to the pool and the waterfall. It is early morning. The sun has barely risen, and it shares the sky with a still visible moon. The dew sparkles, and as you gaze across the pool to the edge of the forest, you notice a shifting of shadows. A breeze brushes across you. You catch the faint sound of a soft tinkling of bells.

You stand, as the air around you seems to become almost electrical. At the edge of the woods, the light shimmers, and there steps from the woods a beautiful unicorn. The early morning light gives it a silver shimmer, and the alicorn radiates a rainbow pearlescence. Its eyes fix upon you, and then slowly it turns toward the woods again. It pauses at the edge and then slowly walks into the shadows.

There is no doubt that you are being invited to follow, and you step gingerly across the water and head toward the woods. Your eyes do not leave the spot in which you saw the unicorn.

As you step into the woods, the shadows close around you, and although you cannot see the unicorn, you hear

ahead of you the soft tinkling of the bells as it leads you further on. You follow the sound through the thickness of the woods. Then the trees suddenly end. Before you is an open meadow with a winding road through it.

On one side of the road are cliffs and paths down those cliffs to waiting tall ships for travelers wishing to sail the seas to new adventures. The other side of the road is lined with trees. The sky is a deep blue purple, and as your eyes look down the length of the road, it seems to be lost among hills that are the footsteps to a distant mountain. Even from this distance, you can see a winding path spiraling up and around that mountain to what appears to be crystal doors set into the crest of the mountain itself. A few of the travelers upon the road have reached the crest of the mountain.

There are people of all ages, races, and types upon this road. Some are traveling alone, some in groups that are large, while others seem to cluster in twos and threes. You are struck with the idea that these are all humans on the journey of life.

There is a carnival atmosphere. The road is lined with sporadic booths, each with its own unique offering, a map to the top of the mountain, with its own virtues and rewards. Some offer adventures. Some offer eternal youth. Some offer wealth and fame, and still others offer excitement and prosperity.

Many of the people wander from booth to booth. Some choose immediately, knowing what they wish. Others stop, listen for a while, and then move on. Some of the booths try to help the travelers, offering advice and maps,

but many people seem to be returning from their trips weary and discouraged.

In the distance, near the first bend in the road, you see the unicorn that led you here. It stands within the middle of the road. Some people see it, but most do not, passing by without a glance. Their attention is upon booths that offer quick and easy routes to the distant mountain.

As the unicorn stands amidst the people upon the road, a light begins to shine around it. The very air surrounding it shimmers like heat off of the road on a hot summer day. There begins to manifest a figure, tall and stately, next to the unicorn. Some travelers stop at this figure's appearance, but most do not even realize the phenomenon.

The unicorn bows slightly to this figure dressed in robes of silvery white, capturing the light and shimmer with each movement. Over the heart is a circular black and yellow patch. The embroidered head of a unicorn, in the same brilliant silver white as the robe, occupies the center of the patch.

This being looks about at the travelers and booths. He frowns slightly at those who offer false wares. He greets the various travelers as they walk by. Some stop, while others do not even respond, completely ignoring his presence and that of the unicorn.

As you approach, a small group has begun to gather. Some are travelers alone on the journey, others in pairs or small groups. As you draw closer, this being fixes you with his eyes, and there is recognition. In that moment you realize that this is the one the ancients called Auriel, the

tallest of the archangels, with eyes that can see across eternity. He nods and smiles softly and lovingly at your perception. And you take a seat with the others before him.

Auriel also sits, and the unicorn reclines, laying its head upon this being's lap. He gently lays his hand upon the unicorn's head. Auriel looks at you and the others warmly and silently at first. Then you hear the voice of this magnificent being filling your heart.

On the journey of life, it is the journey itself that brings our rewards, not the reaching of the summit. For each of you the path will be different, but there are many paths. Remember to be patient with yourself. There is no such thing as instant knowledge or awareness. Illumination may have its sparks, but it is a journey of many steps. We are each building for an eternity, not a lifetime, and an eternity of wisdom takes an eternity of time.

All that you have learned and all that you can do and all that you have experienced are merely tools to assist you in that part of the journey still ahead of you. The tools and the gifts that you acquire along the way are not an end in themselves. You seek the spiritual, but at times you forget that what is psychic is not always spiritual. What is occult or hidden is not always uplifting. And what is desired is not necessarily useful. And yet every dream helps move you along the path. Now see the steps that have led you here and where they may lead in the future.

Auriel pauses, and his fingers softly touch the unicorn's horn. A light begins to emanate from it, forming a growing, circular spiral of energy above you. As you watch, images arise within that circle of light. Images of your past begin to crystallize. You see yourself as a child and as an adult, and the dreams that you have had—the passions that you have had—but did not act upon. You see the ideals you wished to pursue, only to step away from that pursuit to easier and safer paths. You see the dreams you have had in the past year that you have been hesitant to act upon. You see the opportunities that presented themselves to you and upon which you did not act. And then the images shift.

You see the influence of those who inspired or awakened a sense of wonder in you. You see the times in which you acted on your desires, in spite of the fears—sometimes successfully and sometimes not. You see yourself shining more strongly at all of those times. You see the times you acted with courage and succeeded. You see the opportunities that presented themselves and which you acted upon with success. You see the people who encouraged you to follow your heart. And each time you see your light grow stronger around you.

And then the images shift again. You see new opportunities arising in the future. Some are mundane, and others more spiritual. You see new people and new relationships unfolding. You see these people and situations stimulating new dreams and passions. Opportunities to manifest these new dreams, along with some of the old ones, increase in your life. And you see yourself shining even more brightly than ever.

Then these images and the light from which they came forth fade. Both Auriel and the unicorn are now standing before you. Auriel holds within his hand a cup

Ted Andrews

in the shape of a unicorn horn. Auriel looks at you with great love and promise, and he speaks again.

All life brings choice, but choosing does not mean that you lose opportunities. Opportunities are never lost. Dreams are never lost. Hold onto your dreams and remember that whatever path you choose, you will encounter that which will help you grow. Open your heart and follow your dreams. Your life will be filled with wondrous opportunities and joys. Now drink deeply of your dreams.

Auriel extends the cup to you. Each of those present drink of it in turn. You take it within both hands and drink fully the sweet nectar. It sends shivers of delight through your body. You close your eyes reveling in its effect. Every cell begins to sing with new life and possibilities. Your heart is filled with the reality of hope and promise.

As you open your eyes, the scene is gone. You are no longer upon the road. There are no booths or travelers. There is no unicorn and no Auriel. The only sign of the experience is the sweet taste that still fills you with promise. But you do not need to see them to know their reality. You realize that even though your life journey has been years, it has been all preparation. Now the Holy Quest truly begins. And a soft tinkling of bells washes over you in response to this thought. And your heart fills with joyful anticipation for that which will unfold in the days ahead.

Notes

CHAPTER 7

The Unicorn's Companions

Garland the bright horn with
wild, sweet flowers,
...leave him to frolick
alone in the pasture,
Endure the hot longing of this summer day.

Francis Lucien
Allegories

The Unicorn's Companions

For a long time I have worked in the animal program at a local nature center and I serve as one of their trail guides for touring groups. I love to do nature programs with pre-schoolers. First, I don't have to walk very far with them, and second, I don't have to get real botanical.

What I normally do is take them along a trail that has a variety of fairy mounds and such. Along the way, I do some storytelling and talk about some of the fairy lore associated with trees and flowers. On one of these occasions, I stopped at a mound and I was explaining to the group that mounds like this were once called fairy mounds, and that people all over the world believed that fairies and other beings lived inside them. Some of them thought it was cute as I talked, but most of them weren't buying it, or were afraid to show they were because of the teachers and parents present. In fact, one little boy stepped up from the back with his "you-can't-fool-me" look.

"Well, how do they get in and out of there then?" he asked, thinking that he had me.

I smiled and said, "Some people believe they come in and out through the bottoms of the trees nearby."

At that moment, a young girl stepped forward and said, "They do not! They use those little flowers there, there, and there." And she proceeded to point out the different flowers. The adults grinned and rolled their eyes at each other. The girl's mother went white. And inside, I was jumping up and down with joy, yelling, "Yes!"

Throughout the rest of the trail, though, that boy and girl never budged more than a foot from my side. Finally they had encountered an adult that was aware of what they had known about but couldn't discuss with other adults.

On this same hike, I took the group across the nature center's pond boardwalk. I had all of the kids lay down on the boards and I then told them, "If you tickle the water with your fingers, sometimes the water fairies will come out, riding on the backs of dragonflies." Then I lay down next to the kids and we tickled the water with our fingertips. When we

CHAPTER 7

stood up, there were close to a hundred dragonflies circling us. The kids were ecstatic—as I was. The teacher and parents looked at me oddly, and I just shrugged at them. It was a truly great day! For no matter what the kids would be taught from that day forth, I knew that there would forever be a part of them that would know the truth and would always believe.

To experience the unicorn or any aspect of the Faerie Realm, we have to first of all be open to that experience, to keep the child within us alive, to see with a child's eyes and feel with a child's heart. We have to remember that the natural world still contains ancient enchantments. If we enter that space with a sense of sacred wonder and know what to look for, we will encounter things we have only dreamed of.

The quest for the unicorn is more than the seeking of this fantastic creature. Yes, the quest will lead to that, but it will also lead us to so much more. We will begin to experience the phenomenal world of nature in new and magical ways, encounter trees that speak and caverns that lead to nether realms, meet creatures, both natural and phenomenal, that will forever awaken a sense of wonder within us.

In many ways, the quest for the unicorn is the quest for the return of our lost wonder at life, and on that path there will be many fantastic encounters. Each encounter encourages us and urges us on, each encounter reminds us we will succeed, each encounter reminds us the journey itself brings the rewards, not the end of the journey itself.

The unicorn is only one of the guardians of the forest, sharing its guardian's role with many other creatures of the forest, including those humans have relegated to the realm of fiction. We should come to know those, for the more we know about them, the more we will recognize the environments leading us to what we truly seek.

In Chinese lore the unicorn was one of four sacred beasts aiding in the creation of the universe, sharing this task with the dragon, the phoenix, and the tortoise. When the task was completed, each went to their respective realms. The dragon took to the seas, the phoenix to the sky, the tortoise to the swampy wetlands, and the unicorn to the forests, yet the connection between them remained (and still remains) very strong. Because of this relationship, one of the wonderful rewards we experience when seeking the unicorn leads to encounters the other sacred beasts!

Throughout the world there are myriad tales and myths associated with these four sacred beasts. Having many things in common, these fantastic creatures:

- embody and stimulate creative power,
- represent composites of many animals,
- awaken great sensitivities in us,
- stimulate the creative imagination,
- amplify our instinctive intuition,
- appear in a variety of sizes, forms, and colors,
- remain reclusive, so encounters are rare,
- shatter all perceptions—pleasantly,
- serve as guardians to Nature and the Faerie Realm, and
- open us more fully to the hidden wonders of nature.

The more aware we are of these fantastic creatures, their characteristics, and their connection to the unicorn, the easier it is to recognize them in our encounters. Like unicorn encounters, those with the other sacred beasts are often very subtle, but nonetheless, very real. Sometimes these encounters happen as a prelude to the unicorn encounter, sometimes they happen afterward—but happen they will!

DRAGON

IDENTIFYING FRAGRANCE: basil

COMMON FORMS: snake, dragonfly,
firefly, salamander,
lizard, hawk

*Chinese
Dragon*

Like the unicorn, the dragon is one of the most multi-faceted creatures. Its significance is quite complex. Though Christianity and the western world has made the dragon out to be an evil reflection of the devil, it is truly the epitome of great primal power. Unlike in the West, this great power was honored and revered in the East.

Like the unicorn, the dragon has been depicted as a composite of other animals. As with all of the four sacred beasts, it has been known to take various animal forms. It has been the source of many creation myths around the world. If nothing else, these tales reflect the tremendous power and universality of the dragon.

The dragon embodies the forces of wisdom, strength, and spiritual power as well as the primal power of creation. You will begin to have greater strength and protection in your life when you encounter a dragon. Dragons are truly wondrous creatures, and one of the great rewards of working with the unicorn or touching the Faerie Realm on any level is encountering a dragon.

The dragon came to be the explanation for much of the unexplained phenomena of nature, and it has always been linked to the doings of the

Chinese Dragon

earliest gods and goddesses who were powerful, changeable, and contradictory. Just like the unicorn, nothing about the dragon is simple.

Dragons are found throughout the natural world if we know what to look for. They come in a variety of shapes and sizes, and they have been called by myriad names. To the Chinese, dragons were the ultimate power. They could be as tiny as a silkworm or grow to fill the space between earth and the heavens at will. They controlled the climate and weather of na-

---

TRADITIONAL SIGNS OF THE PRESENCE OF DRAGONS

- Fjords, rapids, and waterfalls are "Dragon Gates." Note the association of waterfalls with the dragon as well as the unicorn.
- Thunder and lightning are the realm of the dragon and heat lightning in the summer is often an indicator of a dragon's presence.
- Areas with caves are frequently homes of dragons.
- Volcanic areas often reflect the presence (past or present) of dragons, especially if the volcano is active.
- Whirlwinds, especially those that carry heavy objects aloft, reveal the presence of dragons.
- Waterspouts at sea are signals of a water dragon.
- Smoking holes in the ground and steam rising reveal where dragons emerge for their flights.
- We cannot usually see dragons, especially when they rise to the sky, but wind and rain helps them achieve height. When wind and rain rise suddenly and unexpectedly, it is often the result of dragons.
- Many clouds are formed by the breath of the dragon and they often appear in the sky as clouds. In fact. sudden tempests and thunderstorms often reveal the dragon's presence.
- Areas of heavy mist and fog called dragon's breath are frequented or lived in by dragons.
- Dragons are found where children are free to enjoy the wonders of nature.

---

ture or of one's life. Occasionally when I teach, at the end of seminars on magical dance, a variation of an ancient dragon dance ritual is performed. Usually within three hours (if not sooner) there is a change in the weather. If it's been sunny, it rains or snows. If it has been raining or snowing, it clears and becomes sunny.

Dragons, by nature, are a paradox, and like unicorns, they are very reclusive. They require large amounts of wilderness (land or sea) to live, and with the increasing disappearance of natural lands, their presence upon land has become even more remote, their sightings more obscure.

There are still ways to recognize their presence if we know what to look for. Their presence is often indicated by the sudden wisp of basil fragrance within the air and in areas where basil grows wild. This is especially true for the basilisk form of the dragon. Dragons are also likely to be found where there are caves and in natural circular areas—woods, meadows, and lakes and in environments that are still a little wild and free. When we encounter their signs, the unicorn will not be far away. And when we encounter the unicorn, the dragon will be around the next bend.

PHOENIX

IDENTIFYING FRAGRANCE: myrrh

COMMON ANIMAL FORMS: pheasant, peacock

The phoenix is the great bird of rebirth. Like its companions the unicorn, dragon, and tortoise, the phoenix is a mixture of different ani-

mals with complex significance. In China, the phoenix represented the empress and was married to the dragon, which represented the emperor. It is the sacred animal which rules all feathered creatures.

In the western world, the phoenix is the bird that sacrificed itself to fire and then rose from its own ashes often found within western myth. In Egypt, it was linked to the worship of the sun god Ra who died every night and was born again the next morning. In Christianity, it is a symbol of the death and resurrection of Jesus. Many legends and myths contain common threads that link heroes to this creature. The hero lives a long life, and then the phoenix appears either just before or just after the hero's death. The hero is thus born again.

The phoenix is the symbol of the sun and resurrection, of life after death, a symbol of the immortal soul, love, and eternal youth. In its form as the peacock, it guards of the forest for the unicorn.

As with most of the fantastic creatures, when we seek out one, we always encounter the others. For many people the phoenix is one of the easiest to encounter. Myrrh draws the phoenix as well as signals its presence. When the early morning sun is at its peak or the evening sun can be seen, seek the phoenix. Coincidentally, these are times when the pheasant is more active and about, and the pheasant is one of the animal forms that the phoenix occasionally takes.

A phoenix encounter always heralds a time of new beginning, of new life. In our search for the unicorn, a phoenix encounter can signal the beginning of success in that Holy Quest.

THE TORTOISE

IDENTIFYING FRAGRANCE: earthy, musky

COMMON ANIMAL FORMS: turtle

The tortoise has had an amazing history in the world of symbology. While the other four sacred beasts are often considered mythical creatures that have come to embody real aspects, the tortoise is a real animal that has achieved mythical proportions. The hero of many legends, a guide into the Faerie Realm, living in border areas, the tortoise moves solidly and firmly between worlds and dimensions and teaches us to do so as well.

Tortoise markings have great mythical symbology. The Chinese emperor Fu Hsi discussed in Chapter 2 is said to have derived the hexagrams of the I Ching from the markings on the back of the turtle and some of

the stars he saw in the sky. The tortoise can help awaken us to psychic forecasts, particularly in the realm of time.

The tortoise is the symbol of immutability and steadfastness. When encountered during the quest for the unicorn, it reminds us not to become distracted, to stay steadily upon our path to succeed.

Also known as the "horse dragon" and the "dark warrior," the tortoise and its family group is more ancient than any other vertebrate animal. While tortoises are technically more land bound, in mythology and folklore, the words tortoises and turtles were often interchangeable. For our purposes here, we will use the word tortoise, but what applies to the tortoise also applies to the turtle.

The tortoise shell was a symbol of heaven and its underside a symbol of earth; hence, the tortoise indicates a uniting of heaven and earth, spiritual and physical, the Faerie and mundane.

The tortoise, like the unicorn, is also an animal with varying sexual implications. In Nigeria, it was a symbol of the female sex organs and sexuality. To the Native Americans, it has ties to the lunar cycle—again very feminine. Yet, the manner in which its head pops in and out of the shell was often considered very phallic.

When the tortoise shows up in your unicorn seeking, you will find sexual energies strengthened. Keep in mind, though, as will be discussed more fully in the next chapter, this is the creative life force with ties to the physical sexual drive and response, but also spiritual aspects as well. When tortoises and turtles start appearing, you are likely to start feeling the energies of sexuality often linked with the unicorn, but the tortoise helps ground that energy. You find more effective ways of expressing it, usually through something healing or some other mundane expression.

The tortoise also shows up at the time in our quest when we need to remember we are not separate from Mother Nature and all of her aspects, including those relegated to the realm of fiction. Just as the tortoise or turtle cannot separate itself from its shell, neither can we truly separate ourselves from the wonders of nature. In fact, the tortoise or turtle frequently show up when we begin to doubt we will ever connect. It strengthens our desire and reminds us to be patient.

Griffin

IDENTIFYING FRAGRANCE: no specific fragrance

COMMON ANIMAL FORMS: falcon, vulture, golden eagle

Although the griffin is not one of the four sacred animals, it is a fantastic creature of the Faerie Realm with strong ties to the unicorn, a guardian of the forest, particularly the nature spirits within it. The griffin, like the other animals, is usually depicted as a combination of animals. In general, usually part bird and part mammal.

It is interesting to note that all of the fantastic creatures (those considered more mythical) often have this duality to them often serve contradictory roles, depending upon the individual circumstances: "As bird and beast, it is symbolic of heaven and earth, spirit and matter, good and evil, guardian and avenger. As guardian, it is considered protective and gentle; as avenger, it is vicious and relentless."[1]

The griffin is ever vigilant, with a heightened sense of hearing. It is usually found guarding the unicorn environments, where its acute hearing helps warn the unicorn of outside presences.

As with the dragon, the griffin makes itself known through thunder and lightning in much the same way as the dragon, but griffin thunder and lightning occurs suddenly, usually without warning, and then disappears or ends just as suddenly. Heat lightning occurring during visits to secluded nature areas can indicate griffin presence.

If you find yourself in a meadow that seems appropriate for unicorn visits and find a single vulture circling overhead, you have found a good location. Vultures rarely fly without others near. When this occurs, it may be a griffin using the form of the vulture. Encounters with golden eagles can also be magnificent indicators. Remember that everything in nature works together and is interrelated. When we encounter one aspect, we encounter others. When we seek out the unicorn, we are also seeking the other fantastic creatures, and since the unicorn is the most reclusive of all, encounters with the others usually occur first.

NATURAL COMPANIONS TO THE UNICORN

The following animals are also the natural companions to the unicorn, animals most people are typically more aware because they have not been classified as fantastic or mythological. These are the animals of the natural world whose presence can herald the appearance or reflect an environment compatible with the unicorn. The more these animals are found, the higher the probability the unicorn will visit or is already lives there.

---

[1] Ted Andrews, *Enchantment of the Faerie Realm* (St. Paul: Llewellyn Publications, 1993), p. 189.

Some of these animals were discussed briefly in Chapter 2, but here their relationship to the unicorn now will be investigated in more detail.

These animals have certain qualities and characteristics in common. They was always have a tremendous amount of mysticism associated with them throughout the world. They often symbolize creative and fertile energies and have strong sexual aspects attributed to them. They are commonly associated with metamorphosis and change. More importantly, these animals had strong ties to the Faerie Realm in traditional folklore. Beings of that realm are known to take these animal forms, and their appearance in abundance within an environment usually reflects the presence of nature spirits and enchantment.

If we find that we are encountering any of these animals with greater frequency, it often indicates we are becoming more compatible and open to that realm of life. These animals are excellent indicators that our energy is growing more appropriate to even more fantastic encounters, including that of the unicorn. Frequent presence of these animals reveals we are expressing the child in our heart that is truly open to the unicorn experience.

Birds

Birds are frequently associated with the unicorn, lighting upon the alicorn or riding upon its back. Birds have been said to entwine flowers in the mane and tail of the unicorn while it rests.

Some birds are more closely linked to the unicorn than others. The nightingale, often found in the environments where unicorns live, will sing out warnings or even sing it to sleep. Doves appear in greater numbers when associated with the love aspects of the unicorn.

Hummingbirds have strong ties to the unicorn as well. With its long bill and tongue for extracting nectar from flowers, the hummingbird has been called the unicorn bird. In fact, hummingbirds could not live without flowers, and many flowers could not live without the hummingbirds pollinating them.

Unicorns are drawn to meadows of flowers, as are hummingbirds, so they can be found within the same environment. Hummingbirds are extremely playful, sometimes seeming to be fighting with each other, although no one seems to get hurt. When I have observed these "fights," I am reminded of tales of the unicorn and the lion, often depicted romping, chasing, and play fighting with each other—although in some of the tales, the fighting becomes serious. Hummingbirds have become symbols of sexuality and joyfulness, for accomplishing what seems impossible. They have great speed and the ability to move in ways that also seem impossible. All of the attributes of the hummingbird have also been attributed to the unicorn.

pheasant

Of all the birds, though, the peacock and the pheasant have the strongest ties to the unicorn, as they are forms of the unicorn's companion, the phoenix. The peacock often associated with resurrection, rebirth, and watchfulness. For most people, its eerie call and its feathers, with their blue-green iridescence and what appear to be "eyes," are the two most notable characteristics of the peacock. In Greek mythology, Argus of a Hundred Eyes was a watchman for the goddess Hera. When he fell asleep on duty, Hera punished him by killing him and placing his eyes in the feathers of the peacock.

peacock

Of all the birds, the peacock most completely resembles images of the traditional phoenix, particularly the Chinese form. In Egypt, the peacock was second only to the Ibis in its ability to kill poisonous snakes, linking the peacock to the healing qualities of the unicorn and its wondrous horn. We cannot help but notice the connection between a peacock killing a poisonous snake and those tales of the unicorn cleansing a stream after a serpent has loosed its poison into it. The peacock, because of its watchfulness and guardianship, is one of the great protectors of the unicorn and its home. If intruders enter a unicorn's forest, a peacock will sound its eerie call for warning. If you hear a peacock while wandering in a wood, a unicorn may be nearby or even reside there.

The pheasant is frequently associated with the phoenix as well, especially in unicorn environments. Earlier I spoke of the magical aspects of border areas, *'tween places*, where it is easier to experience beings and creatures of the Faerie Realm. Pheasants live naturally at the edges of woods and fields and are often seen in the wild at powerful 'tween times, dawn and dusk.

Like peacocks, pheasants have beautiful tail feathers, linking them to the phoenix. The tail plumes of the pheasant are often associated with greater expression of sexuality. The search for the unicorn will awaken the sexual energies, our creative life force, becoming stronger and more intensely felt by ourselves and those we encounter. When the pheasant shows up, it is a sign we have tied into the archetypal energies of the unicorn and its sexual aspects. Meditating with pheasant feathers can help us learn how to handle the more intense life force stimulated by the unicorn.

Butterflies

Any encounter with the subtler dimensions of life, even the mere seeking of these dimensions, will stimulate transformation. Many of the animals associated with the unicorn are animals show great transformation, especially the butterfly.

Unicorns love flower meadows, which also draw butterflies. Butterflies dance within meadows—with and about the unicorn. In fact, butterflies and unicorns are almost inseparable. Rarely will you see a unicorn without also seeing butterflies dancing and lighting upon it. When seen together, it appears as if someone has tied flowers into the mane of the unicorn. While some birds do entwine flowers in the unicorn's mane, often what is seen are the vibrant colored butterflies resting upon the unicorn.

Butterflies, like their friend the unicorn, are symbols of change, joy, and color. Both are reminders that transformation in any area of our life can be as gentle and joyful as we wish. It is entirely up to us. Together they remind us to keep our joy alive.

Deer

The unicorn is a close friend of deer and often walks amidst their herds. Many people have done double takes when they have caught sight of a unicorn in a herd. Unfortunately, most of the time they convince themselves that their eyes must have been playing tricks on them.

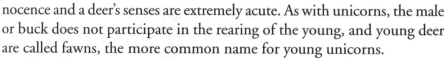

The unicorn and the deer share many qualities in common, so it should not be surprising that they are often seen together. Like the unicorn, deer embody the quality of gentleness and innocence and a deer's senses are extremely acute. As with unicorns, the male or buck does not participate in the rearing of the young, and young deer are called fawns, the more common name for young unicorns.

Deer, like the unicorn, have often captured the imagination. The hunt of the deer was what led individuals away from civilization back to more primal environments. When deer show up in your life, it is time to gently return to your more innocent beliefs and ideas. If you happen to see a small herd of deer, look closely. You may be surprised to see a unicorn walking among them.

Dragonflies

The unicorn has been a dynamic symbol of the power of light, a quality shared by the dragonfly and its realm.

Both the Japanese and the Native Americans speak of a time when the dragonfly was truly a dragon. One of the things we uncover when we open to the subtler realms of life is that many of our preconceptions are shattered. Dragons can be as tiny as a dragonfly or large enough to fill the skies.

Dragonflies, as with all insects, go through metamorphosis. Again, we see the link between the unicorn and the dragonfly through change and transformation. Dragonflies spend about two years in what is termed a *nymph* stage, living in the water before coming out. Correspondingly, the quest for the unicorn may take two years before we see results.

As mentioned in Chapter 2, the pearlescence of the alicorn resembles the pearlescence of the dragonfly. Structures in the shell of the dragonfly refract the light, giving them an iridescent and often rainbow hue, and the same process seems to occur with the alicorn. Since the dragonfly is related to the dragon, it is not surprising it would also have certain qualities in common with the dragon's companion, the unicorn.

When dragonflies appear in great numbers, several things will occur within your life. You will find your activities more protected, your vision will become sharper, and you will start to see the hidden wonders of the natural world, often reflected by encounters with beings of the Faerie Realm. When the dragonflies show up, you are about to see some goal or dream you have worked toward for approximately two years begin to manifest.

The dragonfly inhabits the world of water and of air found around ponds, streams and creeks. If found in abundance near a waterfall, pay particularly close attention. The dragonfly can lead you to the waterfalls of the unicorn. The unicorn is about to step into the light within your life.

Turtle

As one of the sacred companions to the unicorn, the tortoise family has already been examined, and attributes of the turtle as well. Turtles are often seen basking on rocks in streams and pools frequented by unicorns. Granted, turtles can be found doing this in many areas, whether unicorns live there or not. When the other elements and companions also appear within that same environment, then the probability is greater. The turtle is just one of several factors that reflect the presence of a unicorn.

Turtles also show up with great frequency during our quest if we are pressing too hard. Turtles are slow and steady. Long life and groundedness are associated with them. If they begin to appear with greater frequency, ask yourself some questions. Am I going overboard in my searching? Am I being impatient? Am I forgetting that the unicorn must ultimately come to me?

When turtles show up, though, you will soon start to experience the unicorn more strongly through some of the senses. Turtles have a keen sense of smell, and if they show up during your seeking, you will probably start to catch the fragrances indicating the unicorn that has been nearby. The scent of apple blossoms will surround you at times of the year when apple blossoms are not in bloom. You will seem to walk through clouds of cinnamon.

Turtles also have a strong hearing, sensing vibrations through their skin and through their shell. If unicorns are nearby and you are encountering turtles, you will also start to have auditory confirmation of the unicorn's presence. Listen closely. You may hear a peacock calling out its warning to the unicorn. You will hear the song of the nightingale. And you will catch a soft tinkling of bells upon the breeze.

Although these are not visual encounters, they confirm you are on the right track, that your seeking is not in vain. If you are patient and grounded, you will eventually encounter and experience the unicorn fully—through all of the senses.

CHAPTER 7

The Unicorn Boy

BENEFITS
- strengthens friendships
- reveals true perspectives in relationships
- uncovers trust and deception
- enlists the aid of others in your quests or tasks
- strengthens trust in love
- heals past relations

This is an exercise to strengthen our connection to the companions of the unicorn and help recognize their presence. It is a magickal storytelling. The tale is adapted from an Indian epic called *The Mahabharata* (circa 200 BC), which means *great story* in Sanskrit.

I have used variations of this tale in several kinds of exercises, in my own magical dance work, and I have incorporated aspects of it into my "Dance of the Unicorn," which helps align more personally with the unicorn energies. I have used it when teaching shapeshifting, especially when working to align more fully with the fluid energies of the Faerie Realm.

Used in the manner described in this exercise, this magickal story, accomplishes several. You will recognize the signs reflecting the presence of a unicorn and you will become more attuned to the companions of the unicorn and enlist their aid in your quest.

In the week that follows, you will uncover much about your relationships. You will find information unfolding, revealing whom you can trust and whom you cannot. You will unfold clues that reveal deception in friendships and reveal more personal relationships. You may even uncover clues as to where you have jumped to the wrong conclusions.

Opportunities will arise to strengthen old relationships and to develop new ones, to heal riffs of the past, to find you also manifest to test your own trustworthiness. Confidences may be shared more freely with you.

Remember that the unicorn is a creature of tremendous trust and innocence. It demands both from those who would seek it. Betrayal is the greatest thief of childhood trust and innocence. Such losses are extremely difficult to replace. For many, it is a wound to the heart. To heal a wound of such magnitude requires a compassion beyond emotions, a compassion equal to the power of the Grail itself. And this holds great responsibility.

1. The effects of this exercise are enhanced by certain preparations.

    *   As a prelude to the exercise, perform the stances for the sacred beasts of the dragon, phoenix, and tortoise as described earlier in Chapter 3, Exercise 3.

    *   You may wish to do this in a triangulation around the central area in which you will perform this exercise. In the center of this triangle, perform the simple dance of the unicorn. Move from the horse stance to the unicorn posture.

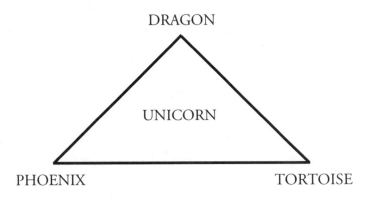

DRAGON

UNICORN

PHOENIX   TORTOISE

2. Use the same Opening and Closing Scenarios as described in Chapter 3, Exercise 4, and use the following magickal story. This is a powerful but subtle exercise, and you will be surprised at the effects it unfolds for you.

3. Remember to read this story through several times to become familiar with it.

CHAPTER 7

MAGICKAL STORY:

THE UNICORN BOY

You are sitting next to a pool in the open meadow. The sound of the waterfall is soft and soothing. A soft breeze brushes across you, and you hear the soft sound of tinkling bells within it. The sunlight sparkles off the surface of the pool, and as you gaze upon it, you see the image of a unicorn rising within the waters. The unicorn appears to be looking out from this pool. As you gaze upon it and into its eyes, the meadow begins to fade from around you.

You see yourself now standing at the edge of a river. On the opposite side of this river is a hut and you see an old man working around it. Though you are standing in the open, he doesn't see you at all. It's as if you do not exist to him. But he exists for you, and as you watch him, you feel the strength of his life. With each passing moment, you seem to know more and more about him.

You know that this man is Kasyapa and that he lives alone. You know that he is a Hindu holy man. You even know that by his own choice, he left the civilized world to live alone in the wilderness of the ancient forests.

Then, to your amazement, you see a beautiful unicorn doe step from around the back of the hut. A soft golden glow surrounds her, and you watch as the old man speaks softly and lovingly her. The doe nuzzles his hand affectionately, and the golden glow about her grows stronger. She raises her head and looks across the river in your direction. You are not sure at first if she sees you or not, but the golden light around her grows stronger still. Then the appearance of the doe begins to change.

For a moment, in place of the doe, stands a beautiful maiden, her hands softly folded over her swollen stomach. You realize she is with child. Her eyes fix upon you for a moment and she smiles at you. Your heart jumps. You feel such strong love coming from her. The blood rushes to your head and you feel yourself blacking out.

As your eyes open, you are bewildered and confused. The bright light of the sun is gone. In the air is the smell of a cooking fire. As you look up, you see the gentle, worn face of the old man. Several tears run down his cheeks. And you realize that he is holding you—that you are a child in this holy man's arms.

You look across the room and there on the bed is the young maiden. Though the light is strong around her, a part of you knows there is no life left. As you gaze upon her, her image changes, becoming the unicorn doe once more and then she also fades into the golden light. And the bed is empty.

You feel something wet upon your forehead, and it begins to tingle. You turn your head to gaze into the eyes of the old man. You realize that it is his tear that fell

upon your forehead. And the old man's eyes widen as the tear brings out of your forehead a single horn. Although you cannot see it, you feel it growing from your forehead.

The old man raises you up above his head and calls out, "This is my son. He shall be called Risharinga, antelope horn."

You see yourself growing up in the ancient forests with the old man. Except for the single horn growing from your forehead, you appear as human as anyone else. But you are different. You feel things more strongly. You see things that others would not see, and with the guidance of the old man, you come to know the forest unlike anyone ever before. You are at one with nature. You understand the language of the animals and you learn how to make life grow. You learn to work with the forces of nature.

In the world beyond the forests, the people and land were experiencing a great drought. Life was drying up and dying. The king in the world beyond was in great distress for it was his own misdeeds that had caused the drought. Of this you are unaware, for all seems right with your world.

The king's advisors had heard of the forest and the child within it who could make things grow, and they told the king. They also warned the king the child of the forest could see what other humans could not and so great care would be needed to lure the child from the forests to the outer world.

The king thought long and hard upon this, and finally asked to speak with his beautiful daughter. He told her of the forest child, and since all humans fell under the spell of her beauty, why wouldn't this child. The daughter did not like the idea of deceiving anyone, but the people were dying. She agreed.

For weeks she sailed up and down the river through the ancient forest, looking for this strange person. She was amazed at how green and beautiful the forest was. It made her realize how even more desperate conditions were in the outer world. Each night she would sail further in, and during the day she would walk and explore, hoping to encounter this mythical forest child. And all the time she is being watched from afar.

Her beauty stirred your heart in so many ways, and finally you realize that just watching her is not enough. You must develop the courage to approach her, and as you walk out of the woods and into the meadow in which she wandered, she catches her breath. It's true! Her eyes widen, and she stares at the single horn growing from your forehead. Only when she sees how her staring makes you feel awkward does she pull her eyes from the horn.

Over the following days, you walk the woods together, you telling her about the animals and she telling you about the outer world. It isn't long until you realize you are truly in love with this beautiful maiden. Although she finds the horn unusual at first, she soon sees past it and realizes just how strong and handsome you truly are.

Then one month to the day that you first spoke to her, she places a small wreath of flowers over your horn and professes her own love to you. Before long you are talking about going back with her to the outer world.

Ted Andrews

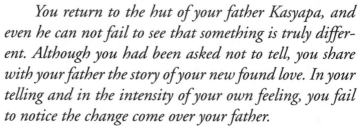

You return to the hut of your father Kasyapa, and even he can not fail to see that something is truly different. Although you had been asked not to tell, you share with your father the story of your new found love. In your telling and in the intensity of your own feeling, you fail to notice the change come over your father.

His face clouds. "This can not be! You cannot be with the outer world. It is not what you think. You are being deceived!"

You are shocked. Never have you seen your father angry. You are confused. Why would he not be happy at your own happiness. And in your shock and confusion, you run.

When you reach the river, the king's daughter sees your distress. She holds you and listens without saying a word as you describe your father's reaction. And her heart begins to ache over her deception. All that she can say is, "It will all work out. It will all work out."

You walk onto the boat, your hand in hers, and as the boat pushes away from the shore, she holds you, not saying a word. Her heart is torn between her love for you and the need to maintain the deception to save the land of her people.

Only when the boat has sailed beyond the borders of the ancient forest does she speak. She cups your face in her hands and speaks softly to you.

"Your father is right. There is deception. I was sent here by my father the king to lure you with my beauty away from the forest to the outer world. The outer world

is dying, and you were our only hope. But when I got to know you, I also came to love you. Though my reason for coming was false, my love is not."

You stare at her wide-eyed. Your hand clutches at your heart. Never have you known there can be such deceit. You begin to understand why your father has warned against the outer world for all these years.

The king's daughter sees your innocent heart breaking and she begins to weep.

"I had to do it for my people. They are dying. Look about you, Risharinga. Look at how our land has withered upon us!

Slowly, you pull your eyes from hers, and as you look about, you gasp. Trees are withered and lifeless. Branches, like old skeletons, extend out to you, pleading. The earth is dry and cracked, and you can see that even the river was coming to an end. The devastation is immense.

There is such sadness at the devastation, your first tears begin to flow. As you weep, a soothing rain begins to fall. The river beds begin to fill. The trees and ground drink of the rain. Flowers begin to work their way from the soil once more. Leaves begin to cover the trees. It is as if the earth is drinking in new life and is being born anew.

You begin to understand. You look at your love, and you see her as you first saw her with the eyes that see beyond the surface. You see her heart filled with love and gratitude. And you embrace.

And the images begin to fade from around you. You find yourself sitting next to the pool by the waterfall. You are gazing into the pool itself. You see the images of a wedding within that pool. You and the king's daughter are being married. Upon her head is the crown of her father, who gave it up because of the shame. Upon your horn is the wreath of flowers she made for you out of love. Behind you stands your father, Kasyapa, and as these images fade, you see the reflection of the unicorn upon the surface of that pool.

As you raise your eyes, you see the unicorn standing upon the opposite side of the pool. A soft golden glow surrounds it and its eyes look upon you with great love and promise. It then turns and walks from the meadow into the woods beyond. And the rest of the images fade from around you.

Notes

CHAPTER 8

The Alchemical Mysteries

*The tortoise, unicorn, phoenix and dragon are all
creatures with counterparts within the human body. All
are called Ling, which means "transcendental." The
tortoise enjoys this earth without haste, and as a result,
lives for a very long time; born of the Earth, the unicorn
is much loved by women, and though rarely found, his
horn is always hard; the phoenix is born from the ashes of
Earth and rises constantly; the dragon, though originally
resting in the bowels of the Earth, hides in the Heaven.*

Nik Douglas and Penny Slinger
Sexual Secrets
p. 159

The Alchemical Mysteries

When people think of alchemy, they usually think of medieval scientists working on secret and exotic formulas in their archaic laboratories to either turn lead into gold or to create an elixir of life. While many of the early alchemists may have actually been doing so, the process had more to do with spiritual initiation:

> It is generally accepted among students of the esoteric that no person ever acquired a knowledge of the deeper secrets of alchemy unless he became an initiate. Every alchemical process ultimately required the use of spiritual powers to complete the desired transmutation...[1]

Alchemy is the study and application of the process of transmutation. In medieval times, it did involve the chemical science of the time and metallurgy, combined with astrology, religion, mysticism, and experimentation. Most of the early alchemists focused upon the transmutation of common base metals, such as lead, into silver or gold. On another level though, it hinted of the transmutation of the soul—turning the lead of our physical life into spiritual gold.

The key to this transformation was through something often referred to as the *Philosopher's Stone*, a mythical powder, stone, or elixir that could accomplish one or more of three things that became the primary focus of the early alchemists:

- turn baser metals into silver or gold,
- create an elixir for eternal youth and life, and
- endow artificial beings (*homunculi*) with life.

The Philosopher's Stone or Elixir of Life would activate the soul's power and thus change both the psychic and the physical world. It would

---

[1] Robert Chaney, *Transmutation: How Alchemists Turned Lead into Gold* (Upland, Astara, 1969), p. 11.

transmute the lower by uniting it with the higher, often termed the *sacred marriage*.

Like the unicorn, the Philosopher's Stone was a true paradox, a stone. It was of the earth, but not of the earth. It was unknown, yet everyone knew of it. The alicorn, many believed, contained the essence of this Philosopher's Stone. Unfortunately, any animal with a similar horn was killed and its horn used to make elixirs of life. Even today, poachers slaughter rhinos for the horn, which is often ground up, powdered and then sold to treat illnesses.

Alchemy has within it many symbols of birth and initiation and it has been described in many ways. It is the joining of the crown and scepter, the marriage of the male and female, the uniting of the sun and moon. This uniting of opposites is frequently found within esoteric tales, lore, and art. "The Quest for the Holy Grail" is but one of the more familiar examples. This alchemical marriage of opposites is also found within the lore of the unicorn. In fact, the sacred marriage has been depicted in occult art as the uniting of the unicorn and the dragon.

In traditional alchemy, mercury was the critical element. In mythology and metaphysics, mercury was often depicted as androgynous—the male and female combined within a single form. The two-headed dragon served as a symbol for mercury because it is a substance that is neither

---

FAMOUS ALCHEMISTS

Chang Tao-Ling (western China)

Nicolas Flamel (France)

Roger Bacon (England)

Paracelsus (Zurich)

Giuseppe Balsamo (Sicily)

Zosimus (Egypt)

Democritus (Greece)

Jan Baptista van Helmont (Belgium)

Abou Moussah Djfar-Al Sofi, "Geber" (Arabia)

Albert von Bollstaedt (Germany)

Thomas Aquinas (Sicily)

Arnaldo Bachuone (Spain)

Heinrich Cornelius Agrippa (Germany)

Robert Boyle (Ireland)

Edward Kelly & John Dee (England)

solid nor liquid. The unicorn was also used to symbolize mercury because of its combined male and female aspects. The horn was male and the lap upon which it put its head was female. Mercury, two-headed dragons, and the unicorn all reflected and represented the sacred marriage.

This sacred marriage is necessary to give birth, whether physical or spiritual. Most alchemical images have multiple meanings, and unfortunately, many of the early alchemists used their own language and their own associations in describing this process, often leaving us to fill in our own blanks. However, the mystery and the strange dichotomy within unicorn beliefs come to new understanding when we examine them in the alchemical light of sacred quests and the hidden mysteries of sexuality.

Transformation through the Sacred Quest

Our modern quest for the unicorn is similar in many ways to the ancient quest for the Holy Grail, one of the more familiar stories of the hero's path to spiritual transformation. Both the images of the unicorn and the Grail retain a vital magic today. Both touch the spirit and the imagination, both involve journeys into the unknown, both open realms and dimensions removed from normal space and time, and both involve a search for the self. The quest for the unicorn and the grail will trigger major transformations within your life.

When the unicorn appears within our life, it acts as a catalyst for transformations we have either been through or are about to go through. An actual face-to-face encounter or the appearance of a live unicorn is not required for these transformations. Because of its archetypal nature, even the least amount of focus upon the unicorn releases its transformative energy into our life. This focus may be a sudden fascination for the animal, or it may be encounters through pictures, photos, or dreams. We can come across the unicorn's image in myriad ways, and we do so with a frequency that is more than coincidence.

A lifelong fascination with unicorns usually reflects a lifetime of transformation, changes on both physical and spiritual levels. It can reflect that this lifetime is one of greater transformations of the soul—that your life is probably following the pattern and destiny of the hero tales, the journey toward initiation. In hero tales, the hero must prove himself or herself worthy through a journey into the unknown. This worthiness may be established by asking the proper question correctly, by avenging a wrong, by winning the grail, by capturing the castle, by remaining steadfast and loyal in the face of temptation, or through a variety of tasks.

The unicorn is the call to adventure that leads the hero into new journeys across a threshold of adventure where the hero meets the guardian who must be confronted, slain, or conciliated. The hero then journeys through unknown territories, facing tests, and gaining magical helpers. The hero encounters the greatest test and the opportunity for the greatest reward. A sacred marriage occurs and a blessing is received. The hero then returns, and if the journey has been successful, the hero re-emerges, transformed, with something that can restore the world left behind. The hero becomes a citizen of several worlds with the freedom to move and live in both. If the journey has not been successful, it must be undertaken yet again.

If the individual refuses the call to adventure as in the story of Ragged John, we encounter other consequences.

> Walled in boredom, hard work, or culture, the subject loses the power of significant affirmative action and becomes a victim to be saved. His flowering world becomes a wasteland of dry stones and his life feels meaningless—even though, like King Minos, he may through titanic effort succeed in building an empire of renown. Whatever house he builds, it will be a house of death....All he can do is create new problems for himself and await the gradual approach of his disintegration.[2]

---

[2] Joseph Campbell, *The Hero with a Thousand Faces* (Princeton: Princeton University Press, 1949), p. 59.

There are, of course, variations within the hero's tale, but it is a tale of transformation, a sacred quest, a path awakened by those who seek or encounter the unicorn. The alchemical transformations triggered by the unicorn in the sacred quest usually take one or a combination of three forms. Each of these transformations brings its own unique testing upon us:

TRANSFORMATION	FORM OF TESTING
Regeneration and Renewal of Relationships	Discrimination
Redemption and Salvation of Self Worth	Uncontrolled Fancy
Rebirth and Trust in the Higher Self	Test of the Teacher

REGENERATION AND RENEWAL

Regeneration and renewal of relationships applies most specifically to relationships with things outside of ourselves and how they affect our own fertility in life. We begin to see areas of our life that are no longer creative, people in our life who are barren or stifling to our fertility, areas and people no longer productive and beneficial for us. We also see the people and areas of our life that are fertile and beneficial for us, and the opportunity to strengthen these relationships manifest.

With this type of transformation, new opportunities surface, opportunities to give up barren people and situations. There occurs stronger attractions to those who are more of like mind, which brings opportunities to establish new, more fertile relationships. There also arises opportunities to strengthen those relationships that remain fertile and beneficial. A greater passion occurs in all relationships. As with all of the transformations, the choice to act upon the opportunity always lies with the individual.

Regeneration and renewal is often recognized by an increase in sexual energy. This is felt within oneself, but also triggers stronger responses in others. As we will discuss later in this chapter, this transformation reflects a stronger activation of the creative life force, and our sexual energy is one of its physical manifestations.

We begin to see more opportunities clearly, to have doors open to us. We begin to realize we have more choices than what we may have imagined, and what we have imagined is but a fraction of what the unicorn can lead us to. We begin to recognize our choices. We must choose whether to remain in outworn patterns or to give them up so that we may establish newer and more fertile ones.

During this time of the TEST OF DISCRIMINATION, opportunities will manifest in which you can discern reality from illusion, the false from the true, when to act, how to act, where to focus energies, when not to focus energies, whom to believe and trust, and whom not to believe and trust. This test involves recognizing and determining half-truths.

In the early part of our journey, there are always obstacles to be overcome in many forms. The unicorn opens us to many wonders that can be very tempting but are often fleeting as well as tests that are not easily overcome. In life, what ultimately unfolds is determined by the individual's choices. How we discriminate determines whether there is fleeting instant reward or movement toward something more substantial, and this is not always easy to determine. Sometimes it involves trial and error; sometimes it involves remembering the mistakes and similar situations of the past and how they played out for us. When we use the past to guide the present and lead us to a more productive future, we are accessing the full power of discrimination.

The unicorn quest may open us to remarkable manifestations which can be quite difficult at times. We must weigh immediate gratification against long term fulfillment, leading to situations that are cleansing and sometimes very humbling, forcing us to sit back and seem to be at the mercy of other people and situations beyond our control. Here the focus must be fully upon the ultimate goal, not the immediate and transitory events. There are times and places we must take action; there are times and places we must be idle. Discerning when to do each can make the difference between ultimate success and failure. Sometimes it is best to surrender temporarily so that the ultimate prize can be won permanently. Focusing always upon the ultimate goal is the key to success in this transformation.

REDEMPTION AND SALVATION

Although redemption and salvation is a Christian concept, it describes the kind of transformations many individuals experience when they align with any sacred quest, especially of the unicorn or Grail. This kind of transformation involves reawakening and rebuilding self worth, and it will trigger certain definable effects within the normal day-to-day life experience.

We encounter people and situations with whom we have erred. People from our past return so we may correct those previous errors, set them right, or vice versa. It is not unusual for those who have wronged us to return, or for new people similar to those in our past to surface within our life. In some cases, it may be to make amends; in other situations, it may be to learn to handle such situations differently, offering an the opportunity for a retesting of those lessons, promoting the establishment of a new pattern so we neither victimize nor become victims.

Opportunities surface to pursue studies or activities bringing greater individual recognition, to pursue dreams long pushed aside or forgotten. In this transformation, we discover as we follow our dreams and have faith in them, we achieve our greatest successes. We begin to see more clearly how we touch and affect the lives of others and how they touch and affect us. Things said more lovingly are felt more lovingly. Things said more cuttingly, are felt more deeply. We see more clearly the effects we have on others as well as the effects they have on us.

CHAPTER 8

Opportunities surface to discover and explore new aspects of our being, to reconnect with out lost spirit. These aspects may be physical, emotional, mental, or spiritual. This is often the kind of transformation occurring when individuals undergo the shamanic aspect of *soul retrieval*.

In this second transformation, the individual works to reconcile and incorporate the spiritual with the physical, integrating the mystical and spiritual beliefs within the normal day-to-day life. We see aspects of this demonstrated regularly in the metaphysical and psychic field. Unfortunately, many people wrongly assume if they are not actually working within the metaphysical field, they are not truly upon the spiritual or sacred path. Others, with just a rudimentary knowledge may step out prematurely to try and teach and the results may be disappointing. Lacking depth of knowledge or experience to teach in the safest and most beneficial manner, the results may be disheartening and ill-fated. This is part of the TEST OF UNCONTROLLED FANCY.

Uncontrolled fancy is learning to separate the illusions and maya of ourselves from the reality of who we are. Ego comes into play here to a great degree. What is psychic is not always spiritual, what is occult or metaphysical is not always beneficial, what is appealing is not always useful to us. The sacred path does not lead up into some light in which all of our troubles are dissolved.

The sacred path helps us to recognize that through the fulfillment of our daily obligations in a creative manner, we grow and unfold our hidden and sleeping potentials. This transformation involves taking responsibility for one's thoughts and actions—good, bad, or indifferent. For some, the sacred path will take shape by teaching and working in the field of metaphysics and human potentials. For others, it will simply take the form of living the daily life in as creative manner as possible, providing a positive influence of the lives of others.

The actual form of the sacred path does not really matter. One way is neither better nor worse than another, nor one way more glamorous than another. However, if the perception is that one way is better than another, then work needs to be done on uncontrolled fancy. Many believe I live a very glamorous life. It involves writing, which most assume automatically makes me wealthy, even though less than 10 percent of all those who are published are able to actually make a living out of writing. I travel, which many assume is glamorous, not realizing my travel is all work, demands living out of a suitcase for great lengths of time, and being away from home and loved ones. Many believe my success came easily and quickly, when I have been working at this seriously for over thirty years and working to support myself in this field full time for over a dozen years. When our perceptions are far different from reality, we are dealing with uncontrolled fancy.

When we seek the unicorn or pursue any sacred path, our illusions will be brought to light. We may have a vision, but the vision alone is not a guarantee of success. For its manifestation, there must be appropriate preparation and pursuit or the vision will usually collapse. We live in a fast food society, and unfortunately, most people expect the spiritual path to be quick and easy when it requires great effort, strength, patience, and persistence:

> Nothing in the world can take the place of persistence. Talent will not; nothing is more common than unsuccessful men with talent. Genius will not; unrewarded genius is almost a proverb. Education will not; the world is full of educated derelicts. Persistence and determination alone are omnipotent.[3]

Often the occult life assumes a supernormal or supernatural caricature, but the ancient mysteries have always been available to those willing to put forth the time, energy, and effort to find them.

In this second type of transformation, our false glamours will be revealed, whether they are glamours about ourselves, about others, about

---

[3] Israel Regardie, *The Complete Golden Dawn System of Magic* (Phoenix: Falcon Press, 1984), p. 22.

our work, or about our lives. We must face these illusions. We must develop faith and determination in our own abilities and not look to others. As we realize our own self-worth and become confident in our abilities, we begin to achieve. It is easy to become discouraged, but we must remember all who go forth, in whatever manner, will achieve their true aim eventually.

REBIRTH AND TRUST IN THE HIGHER SELF

This third type of transformation which occurs in the quest for the unicorn involves aspects of the other two, but on a slightly different level. The other transformations occur in our own personal search for truth and result from it. This transformation involves the life situations which occur when we challenge the accepted beliefs or traditions. When we dare to doubt the accepted and choose to pursue our own beliefs—for good or for bad—our actions elicit responses in the world around us. This transformation involves leaving one condition to discover a richer and more mature one, and sometimes involves a cleansing and purging of the past— a radical departure.

This is where we face the raised eyebrows and accusations of others. Sometimes it involves ridicule and ostracizing for our beliefs. These situations usually result from others wishing we not change or their refusal to accept our changes. In the traditional hero's path, the individual leaves one condition in order to achieve what is perceived as a better one, committing the self to something bigger or greater.

This transformation always involves a strength-of-will test. In these tests, we find other people—often the ones closest to us—because of their strong wills, have a tendency to control or dominate. They resist our changing and refuse to view us in any manner besides how they have always perceived us. In the past, we may have tended to give in and go along. Part of this test involves deciding in each situation what is right for us and then sticking to it, regardless of how others respond. This is easier said than done, especially when it involves, family, friends, and other loved ones.

Stepping out onto one's own path involves learning to trust one's inner nature and to act upon it. The first step is the most difficult and has been compared to walking upon a razor blade. This first step may be precarious, but with each additional step, the edge widens, becoming a living bridge to new realms. Through this process, we heal ourselves of the habitual patterns in our life, those preventing our growth or those simply outworn patterns no longer beneficial to us.

In some traditions, this stepping is known as meeting the "Dweller on the Threshold." or "Facing the Shadow Self," those aspects of ourselves that we have painted over, glossed over, shoved to the back of the closet, and pretended didn't exist. We must face them, accept ourselves in spite of them, and thereby transmute them. This is the guardian of the hero's path we must each face at some point.

This meeting of the shadow self does not always cleanse the old and integrate the new, but each time we face it, we open to new energies and to new abilities. It stimulates a dynamic period of self-evaluation. We are forced to take a look at the people, the circumstances, and our life situations as they relate directly to who we are and to what we are doing with our life. Meeting the shadow self will stimulate a very emotional time, but whatever is cleansed will be replaced by something much more beneficial to us and where we are going.

The TEST OF THE TEACHER involves learning to trust what we have learned and what we know is best for us. In tales and myths, there is often an older figure—human, animal, spiritual—who provides guidance and assistance along the way. How the hero acts upon the advice or assistance determines the future. The test involves remembering that we take or borrow what we can from whatever source we can and adapt it for ourselves. Or, as it was told to me: "You must stay on the path, but you must also know when to step off the path onto your own."

This testing also involves recognizing that as we are transformed, our new knowledge and abilities grow stronger. With greater strength, there is also greater opportunity for misuse by us and others. It is not unusual to encounter others who have tremendous knowledge, but work for their own benefit. They mix half truths with half lies, and it is here the testing becomes more intense.

At all times it is important to remember to test all things of the earth and of the spirit. Testing helps us to eliminate doubt and develop surety. Those truly for us will not be offended by our testing them, nor should we be offended when they test us. We must remember ultimately no one knows us better than ourselves. The consequences of our action or inaction falls upon our own shoulders. Realizing this and accepting it, we find ourselves re-emerging in our life with renewed confidence, strength, and power. Like the unicorn, although captured, we re-emerge with new life and freedom.

This transformation enables us to look beyond physical limitations to see the creative possibilities that exist within limitation, while at the same time transcending them. We begin to look into ourselves for the answers, for our own magic and miracles. Not from books or from teachers—although they serve their purposes—but from the well of truth and light that lies within us.

The Unicorn and Sacred Sexuality

By medieval times, the unicorn had developed a decidedly Christian tone, but even with this Christianizing, its sexual and sensual aspects could not be ignored. The sexuality associated with the unicorn showed up in art and lore, and the romantic sensuality of it remained strong.

In the 13th century, the image of the unicorn was an image frequently showed up in the work of a poet and songwriter by the name of Thibaut, the Count of Champagne and Brie, and King of Navarre. Thibaut was a religious tyrant who ordered 183 convicted heretics burned to death. He was also one of the best loved songwriter's of the 13th century:

The unicorn and I are one:
He also pauses in amaze
Before some maiden's magic gaze,
And while he wonders, is undone.
On some dear breast he slumbers deep
And treason slays him in that sleep.
Just so have ended my Life's days;
So Love and my Lady lay me low.
My heart will not survive this blow.[4]

During the Italian Renaissance, Bernardino Luini wrote a popular story entitled "Procris and the Unicorn." In this story, Procris is killed by her husband when he heard her moving through the trees and mistook her for a unicorn.

Another popular unicorn story of this same period was written by the Italian poet, Luca Pulci. In this tale, a mortal man falls in love with a wood nymph by the name of Nephele, and in time wins her heart as well. The goddess Diane hears of this romance, and since it is forbidden for a mortal to love a wood nymph, she decides to punish him. She splashes water in his face and he begins to change, turning into a unicorn which hears and understands the voices of animals. He is more filled of the forest life than ever before, but he doesn't realize he has become a unicorn. He soon spies Nephele and he runs towards her. Not recognizing her lover in his new form, she draws an arrow and shoots him. This tale is the basis for the exercise at the end of this chapter.

---

[4] Nancy Hathaway, *The Unicorn* (New York: Viking Press, 1980), p. 18. From *The Unicorn* by Nancy Hathaway. Copyright ©1980 by Nancy Hathaway and Rosebud Books, Inc. Used by permission of Viking Penguin, a division of Penguin Books USA, Inc.

UNICORN WITH WOMEN

*Frequently the unicorn was depicted with women in sensual poses
and varying degrees of undress.*

The Alchemical Mysteries

The unicorn was considered libidinous by nature, partly by its association with wild and primitive people, as savage and naked men and women who were believed to ride upon the backs of unicorns. In the engraving "Rape of Persephone" by Albrecht Durer (1471-1528), he depicts Pluto riding upon the back of a unicorn carrying Persephone off to the underworld. In spite of the Church's influence, the unicorn was never able to be freed of its sensual attributes. When we examine the alchemical aspects of sexuality, we begin to understand why.

In many ways, the West has much to learn regarding sexuality, where it is riddled with guilt and separated from the spiritual. The Christian ethic has deemed the sexual act for creating children, not pleasure, separating the flesh from the spirit and encouraging suppression and denial of sexual energies, although there is still an unconscious recognition of its inherent power. Sexuality continually seeps into the Western culture in spite of its frequent censorship, reflected clearly in examining the art of the unicorn. There are depictions of the unicorn with the Madonna, but there are also paintings of the unicorn with seductive women. If nothing else, this dichotomy reflects the archetypal influence of the unicorn.

There is tremendous hidden and mystical significance to the sexual act. The linking of the male and female is an act of creating wholeness and always brings new birth. When performed within oneself, it gives birth to the Holy Child within. This sacred marriage, when performed with another, can become an earthly expression of the uniting of gods and goddesses, the sun and moon, heaven and earth, the mortal realm with the Faerie Realm, the physical with the spiritual.

The unicorn clearly reflects clearly by this duality. It has the phallic horn, but it is only captured and tamed by the maiden. On one level, it can reflect the animal nature tamed by the higher, spiritual nature. On another level, it can reflect the union of the male and female—the sacred marriage, the marriage of the unicorn and the maiden. The head of the unicorn, with its phallic horn resting upon the lap (or womb) symbolizes the sacred marriage.

CHAPTER 8

To understand the alchemical significance, we must remember that the sexual energies are physical manifestations of more dynamic spiritual forces at play, creative impulses which are the key to the true alchemical process. An ancient pagan ritual involves placing a knife into a cup, symbolizing the union of the Father with the Mother. To put this image in our terms, it is the alicorn in the lap. This pagan ritual is symbolic of the act of creation, or giving birth to a new expression of energy.

In daily life, the male and female often are out of balance. Ritual and ceremonial sex transmute ordinary space and time, imbuing the sexual act with great sacredness and power, creating harmony, becoming an intersection of male and female, day and night, positive and negative, physical and spiritual which are no longer separate, creating a time and space where all possibilities exist. This transmuting of the ordinary to create extraordinary possibilities is the alchemical process, a process greatly determined by the focus of one's thought at the time of the sacred marriage, the time of creation. This is why a unicorn encounter can change one's life and perspective so dramatically.

When the unicorn appears, there occurs a heightened, blending of sexuality and spirit within the individual. This can reveal itself in a wide variety of ways. The sexual drive becomes stronger, more intense. Our sexual responses to others grow stronger and those towards us intensify. Healing is stimulated. Artistic and creative inspiration are heightened. All are tied to the stimulation of the sexual energy, the creative life force, by the appearance of the unicorn.

When we discussed the Eastern unicorn, we talked of tales in which the unicorn would appear to a woman who would become pregnant with a great teacher, a pregnancy not an immaculate conception, but part of the natural sexual act. Sex and spirit, sex and the divine, often occurred together. The various mythologies around the world have tales of gods and goddesses mating with mortals. Even on a superficial level, the symbolism of the blending of the physical and the spiritual through the sexual act cannot be denied!

The spiritual power of sexuality is ingrained in the East. In many Eastern traditions, the sexual energy is honored for what it is, an expression and manifestation of the life force, directly linked to what is termed the kundalini, the serpent energy. It is the creative life force, the force we use and draw upon for everything in the physical and the spiritual worlds. In more modern, scientific realms, it can be aligned with the energy inherent within the DNA molecule, the energy of life. This spiral of creative life force is reflected in the spiral of the unicorn horn.

Ancient traditions recognized the inherent transforming power, physical and spiritual, of sexuality. Tantrism and Taoism are two of the more commonly known Eastern traditions incorporating the sexual energy in ways that can easily heal and transform. These traditions recognize there is more involved in the sex act than mere procreation and genital orgasm. Sexual energy is a powerful and sacred force that can be used to transmute everyday conditions, attitudes, health imbalances, and more:

> Tantra is a cult of ecstasy, a personal religion based on the mystical experience of joy rather than dogma. Sex is holy to a Tantric. It is worship; it is energizing and life giving. Tantric art, writings and religious rituals glorify sex. Tantrics are anti-ascetic; they affirm life. They teach the discovery of the divine through the exaltation of the total human. They use all of the sense, the mind and the spirit to reach mystic peaks.[5]

Threads of this sacredness still exist within the Western unicorn tradition, but they are often overwhelmed by feelings of guilt and shame. The remaining remnants are found in alchemical descriptions, art, and lore. The erotic connections are reminders that we shouldn't—can't—deny the power of sexuality.

---

5 Margo Anand, *The Art of Sexual Ecstasy* (Los Angeles: Jeremy P. Tarcher, 1989), p. 39.

CHAPTER 8

When we see or experience the unicorn, we feel its power. What we feel is what in the East is associated with the activation of the kundalini, the great power inherent within the human organism. We feel an inner thrill, a titillation. Our breath is taken away. There is a sense of electricity, a feeling of lightness and liberation. We experience alternating flushes of heat and cold. Sensuality and even erotic visualization are stimulated. These are some of the tangible signals of our creative life force being triggered by the unicorn.

It then becomes our task to direct and express it appropriately. We must tame it, like the maiden with the unicorn. Only then does it stay alive and become a force we can use to transmute the conditions of our lives.

Notes

CHAPTER 8

EXERCISE 13:   Sacred Sex and the Sacred Beasts

BENEFITS

• harmony, healing
• passion
• transcendence
• sacred union of
  heaven and earth
• strengthening and
  empowering relationships

Imitating the lovemaking of animals has had many mystical and magical aspects to it. In the Orient, it was done to harmonize the elements between heaven and earth. Often eroticism was used to represent and activate various divine forces and expressions of those forces. Sexual arousal is considered the raw emotion of love, used to stimulate passions and to awaken the life force more fully.

That awakened life force, then, can be directed and focused for a variety of tasks, from healing individuals involved to harmonizing and healing the environment. In the latter case, the participants represent divine forces so that their union—their sacred marriage—releases dynamic energies into the living environment where it can be focused and used for inspiration and enlightenment. All depends upon the specific sacred ceremony.

In Taoist and Tantric traditions, various sexual positions will awaken and direct the creative energy along specific avenues. Often these positions are based upon the way specific animals perform the sexual act. The four sacred beasts—the dragon, the phoenix, the tortoise, and the unicorn—have their own sexual positions as well. These positions can be used alone or in alternating patterns, from one to the next, with great effects.

This exercise is most effective when performed in a ritual and sacred manner. Sacred does not mean somber and serious. Lovemaking is pleasurable and should be enjoyed. The sacredness occurs naturally when each participant is honored and respected, and both participants recognize that the sexual act will entwine their energies powerfully and the intimacy will awaken physical and spiritual energies.

It is not the function of this book to teach the many aspects associated with ritual and ceremonial lovemaking. For now it is enough to know that the energy generated can be and should be directed toward a goal that both participants have agreed upon. This agreement raises the sexual act to a level beyond the mundane, opening and linking the spiritual with the physical, the infinite with the finite.

There are, in fact, many kinds and forms of sex rites and ceremonies. In this book, we will focus upon the postures and positions of the four sacred creatures, which balance, harmonize, and heal, giving birth to our relationship on new levels.

CHAPTER 8

PRELIMINARIES

1. Make appropriate preparations. Take the phone off the hook. Make sure you will be undisturbed.

2. Prepare the space where the ritual will be performed.

    *   For most people it may be the bedroom, but it can be any space where both will feel safe and undisturbed. The location should be clean and fresh, and appropriate incense and candles can help enhance the mood.

    *   Have low volume, soft music (no heavy drums or percussion) available. The music is for background only.

3. Food and drink can be a wonderful additive.

    *   The food should be light, not heavy. The participants may want to feed each other as foreplay. Some fruit, crackers, or cheeses will help stimulate without weighing heavily upon the body and mind.

    *   After the ceremony, food can be used to help ground the energy of the participants.

4. Prepare the body.

    *   Bathe and cleanse. The participants may wish to bathe together. Something as simple as this builds harmony, is arousing, and can be wonderful foreplay. Take turns drying each other.

    *   A soft massaging of each other with a fragrant oil can be arousing and heighten the energy.

5. Stand facing each other, and perform the dances to the sacred creatures, as you learned earlier in this book. Perform the dances slowly, mirroring each other. This, in itself, builds harmony and aligns your individual energies.

6. Begin to slowly caress each other and gently move into and through all of the positions.

   • Use the same order you use for the dance. Make the unicorn the last sexual position.

   • Take your time with all of these positions. You may wish to cycle through them several times before the final climax.

7. Don't be afraid to adapt or change.

   • Do what is comfortable for both. Relax and allow yourself to truly enjoy the feelings.

   • Try to maintain as much focus as possible throughout.

SEXUAL POSITIONS

The Turning Dragon

1. The woman lies back, and the man places his knees on the bed between her legs

2. The woman guides the not-quite-erect penis into her vagina. While she does this, the male caresses and strokes her upper body.

3. The male then intersperses two deep strokes between eight shallow strokes.

    • The rhythm is slow and smooth.

    • The man must refrain from orgasm, but the woman may experience satisfaction.

VARIATION: the typical "missionary" position

BENEFITS: overall healing position for both, particularly so for the man if the semen is retained.

The Phoenix

1. The woman lies on her back, raises her legs, and places her feet upon the man's chest.

2. The man kneels between the woman's legs and penetrates her as deeply as possible, alternating three deep strokes with eight shallow ones.

    • The movements should be as vigorous as possible, with the man pressing firmly against the woman's buttocks.

    • The male should refrain from orgasm and bring the woman to climax.

VARIATIONS:

- Instead of kneeling, the man sits, pressing his buttocks against the woman's, with his legs extended along the sides of her body, and movement less rapid.

- The man kneels between the woman's legs. Instead of the woman's feet resting upon his chest, he holds her feet and legs straight up.

BENEFITS: believed to cure one hundred ailments; one of the nine Taoist healing positions.

The Tortoise

1. The woman lies on her back and raises her knees, with the help of the man, till pressed against her chest.

2. The man, on his knees, penetrates from the front, alternating deep and shallow strokes and refraining from orgasm.

3. The male should cease moving entirely when the woman climaxes.

VARIATIONS: The man sits with the woman on his lap, her legs extended over his on either side. Mouth, arms, and body parts touch the corresponding parts of the partner.

BENEFITS: builds longevity; stamina; strengthens the nervous system

CHAPTER 8

The Unicorn

1. The woman lies on her back and lifts her right leg, placing it on the left shoulder of the man.

2. The man kneels as close to the woman as possible and guides himself into her.

    •   The rhythm should be whatever is most enjoyable to each other.

    •   The woman should reach orgasm first; then the man.

VARIATIONS:

    •   Both legs of the woman are placed over the shoulders of the man.

    •   The woman faces away from the man on her elbows and knees, or with her legs straight, the male entering her from behind.

    •   The woman lies down with face, breasts, and stomach against the bed. From behind, the man works under, extending himself flat on top of her, with the woman raising the lower part of her body to assist his movements.

BENEFITS: mutual pleasure and orgasm; pregnancy; balances the elements

Unicorn with Maiden

CHAPTER 8

EXERCISE 14: The Unicorn and the Wood Nymph

BENEFITS

- strengthen love
- clear perspectives on relationships
- transform through love
- heal the past
- break outworn patterns

This exercise is based upon the old tale by the same name, although I have changed aspects of the tale to increase the benefits. It is a good idea to perform this exercise at least two days in a row. On day one, visualize yourself in the role of the individual who falls in love with the beautiful woodland being; on the following day, visualize yourself as the woodland being.

I have tried to make this exercise as non-sexist as possible. The wood nymph in the original story is now a woodland being, so you can visualize it as male or female, whichever you desire. When switching the roles, and you are the woodland being, the mortal (the person of the outer world) can be visualized as male or female.

Performing this exercise in each of the roles elicits different effects. As the mortal who falls in love with the woodland being, you will find in the weeks that follow how other people perceive the changes you are going through. Opportunities to break out of outworn patterns will surface within your life. The choice is always yours, but the opportunities will surface. If you are unready for them, you may wish to avoid this exercise.

When you perform this exercise as the woodland creature, you will begin to see how your life is affecting others around you. Choices will arise as to whether it is time to commit to new patterns and habits or to stay with the old.

This exercise will stimulate the sexual energies in you. You will probably find that others will become more strongly attracted to you, and you will find yourself responding with stronger sexual energies to others as well. In the following week or two, you will find yourself encountering others who are of more like mind to you. New horizons will open.

This exercise also stimulates heightened perception and empathy. You will feel what others are feeling; you will be more aware of how others see and feel you. This exercise can also stimulate greater passion and empathic communication with all of nature, particularly animals. Remember that spirits and woodland beings, not to mention the unicorn, can help open our senses more fully to the wonders of nature.

1. As in the other exercises, make careful preparations.

    • If possible, at some point perform this exercise in the woods.

    • Perform the dances for the sacred creatures. As you complete the exercise for the unicorn, make yourself comfortable, breathe deeply and relax.

2. Allow our opening scenario to unfold. Allow yourself to see and feel the wonders of love about to open for you.

THE UNICORN
AND THE WOOD NYMPH

A scene begins to unfold for you. You find yourself standing within that beautiful meadow that has now become so familiar to you. The sunlight sparkles off the water, and the sound of the waterfall is soothing.

Today you decide to enjoy the green woods at the edge of the meadow. There is a sense of quiet anticipation, as if the woods themselves are waiting for you. You cross the edge of the meadow and step into the woods, and a soft quiet settles around you.

You spot what looks to be a deer path through the thick underbrush, and you follow it. As you walk along, you feel yourself coming more alive. Your can smell the wood and greenery about you. The ground is cushioning, and then you hear something in the distance. You pause, tilting your head, listening more closely.

At first there is nothing, but then…yes…a soft voice, faint and indistinct, but there is no doubt it is a voice. You step further into the woods, pausing every few feet to listen. You realize someone is singing, and it draws you further in into the woods. The song rises and falls in a haunting, enticing manner.

Soon you are standing behind a large tree at the edge of the clearing. In the center of this clearing a small bubbling spring rises out of the heart of the earth itself. In the trees and at the edges of this clearing are a myriad of forest animals, drawn to this spot by the haunting song, just as you were.

In the center of the clearing, you see a figure dancing around the spring, singing the haunting song. This figure has wreathes of wildflowers and greenery upon its wrists and in its hair. The sunlight shimmers off the figure, casting a soft glow.

The figure turns to some of the animals and walks toward them. You are surprised they do not scatter. Then each animal is softly and lovingly touched by the figure. As the figure turns from the animals to face in your direction, your heart jumps and you catch your breath. Never have you seen anything so beautiful! And in that moment you realize this is a being of the woods.

There is such a youthful vitality to this being, and yet the eyes tell you this being is much older than appearances would indicate. It is a primitive wildness you can feel, although it is masked. And you feel twinges of sexual arousal. A part of you would love nothing better than to spend the rest of your life just watching this being dance and listening to its song.

Suddenly you realize this being has seen you. The eyes only hold yours for a moment, and goose bumps rise all over your body. Then the figure turns and darts into the shadows of the woods on the other side of the clearing,

disappearing from your sight. Your heart sinks, and you step from behind the tree into the clearing.

A sadness comes over you. In just those brief minutes, the being had filled your heart. It was like meeting one of your favorite dreams. You look down at the small pool of water. There, in the grass beside the pool, is a small flute. You pick it up and realize it must be the flute of the magnificent being.

You bring the flute up to your lips and tentatively blow on it, making a soft sound. A breeze brushes over you and there is a soft tinkling of invisible bells in the air. You smile. Sitting softly in the grass, you begin to play the flute. You are surprised you are able to do so, and you immediately decide the flute must be enchanted.

With each note, you feel yourself growing more tired, and in just a few minutes you are drifting off into a soft sleep filled with images of people and situations within your life. You see the pattern of your life, and you feel the boredom pressing in upon you. You see the activities and duties you perform daily, not out of love or responsibility, but out of habit. You see the dreams you have had and did not act upon.

Then you begin to see those things you loved as a child and gave you great joy. You see how your own joy affected those around you, lightening and making their days a little better. You see the people who have encouraged you to follow your heart and your dreams, who have tried to show you anything is possible.

Then you see yourself getting older and forgetting your dreams. You see yourself acting more grown up, and you

see your dreams trying to surface so you can capture them once more. Then you see others in your life looking at you peculiarly, as if you've gone a little crazy. You hear voices telling you to grow up, that this is no way for an adult to behave. They tell you to look at what you will be giving up, that this is no time to be chasing rainbows. But there is something strange in their voices. You realize your are hearing fear and sadness beneath their words, and you know there can be no other choice for you.

At that point you wake up, lying in the grass next to that small pool of water in the clearing. You raise your head, and the air smells sweeter and fresher than it has ever before. You seem to be able to distinguish a myriad of smells. The individual flowers, animals nearby, traces of everything within the woods are in the air about you and you recognize them all! You are amazed.

The sounds of the woods are sharper. You hear a mouse moving in the grass 100 yards away. You can even hear the sound of your waterfall beyond the woods. The colors about you are so much brighter. It's as if the dream has awakened your senses for the first time. Never have you felt so alive, so sensual, so vibrant.

You lower your head to drink from the pool, and your eyes widen. Your heart jumps. You close your eyes, shaking your head. Surely this can't be! It must be the light. You open your eyes and stare at your reflection in the pool. What looks back at you is the face of a magnificent unicorn.

You twist your head to look at your body, and you see the white fur and the four legs. You look back to your

reflection, and the horn in the middle of your head shim-
mers, casting a soft glow of light about you.

You jump to your feet and find yourself halfway across
the clearing in that single leap. It is almost as if you were
flying, you are so light, so airy. Never have you felt so free.
You begin to do leaps back and forth across the meadow,
and you begin to laugh. The sound of that laughter be-
comes the sound of soft bells within the breeze.

You walk over to the stream, and leaning over it, you
gaze at your reflection. This time you see your own face
inside that of the unicorn. Then the sound of the flute is
heard, and as you turn to look in its direction, you see the
magnificent being step from the woods into the clearing.

Your heart jumps and you are filled with great love.
As you gaze upon this being, you can see and feel every-
thing it sees and feels. You realize that your love has re-
turned. Ever so softly, this beautiful woodland being ca-
resses your face with a touch that sends shivers through
your body. You lower your head to give this being access to
your horn. With a touch as gentle as a breeze and as lov-
ing as a mother with her newborn child, your alicorn is
stroked from its tip to its base. You shiver and then rear
up, filled with joy, your blood hot and pulsing with new
life.

Then this beautiful being steps back from you and
bringing the flute up, plays a haunting series of tones three
times, and then the flute is laid upon the ground. The air
around this being begins to shimmer, and you watch as
the figure begins to shift and change. Your eyes widen

with joy and surprise as this magnificent being becomes an even more magnificent unicorn before your eyes.

Slowly this unicorn steps toward you and caresses your horn with its own. Again you rear. You are filled with a sense of promise. All truly is possible! The other unicorn seems to smile, and you both swing around and gallop silently into the shadows of the deep forest to share the wonders of the world together. You leave whispers of bells and the fragrance of apple blossom behind as a promise of hope to others who may follow.

CONCLUSION

The Sacred Quest of the Unicorn

JIM: *What kind of thing is this one supposed to be?*

LAURA: *Haven't you noticed the single horn on its forehead?*

JIM: *A unicorn, huh?*

LAURA: *Mmmm-hmmm.*

JIM: *Unicorns, aren't they extinct in the modern world?*

LAURA: *I know!*

JIM: *Poor little fellow, he must feel sort of lonesome.*

Tennessee Williams
The Glass Menagerie
p. 121-122

The Sacred Quest of the Unicorn

The second time I was to see a unicorn would be in the fall of the year I started junior high school. It's interesting how some years stand out in our lives more than others. This would be a year filled with heart ache and disappointment, and yet it would be a year that would bring many revelations and transformations that would sow the seeds and set the pattern for who I am now.

The previous year was one of the best I had ever had. I missed a lot of school due to my asthma and other illnesses, but I also accomplished a lot as well. I received a citizenship award from the school. I was honored for collecting more money for the United Appeal Drive (now the United Way) than any other elementary school pupil in the Dayton area. I made the first basketball team the school had, and in our only game, an exhibition with the other elementary schools, I stole the ball and scored four points. All in all, for a sixth grader at that time, it was a year of major successes.

The United Appeal Drive took up a great deal of school time. While the drive was going on, the school was administering the Iowa Test of Basic Skills. This test would be the basis for how we would be placed in junior high, which, of course, they never told us. Because I was tied up with the drive, I missed a lot of the test, and so I was forced to use recess time to make it up. Being a typical sixth grader, I didn't care to spend my recesses taking tests. The first couple of test sections I completed as I would normally would, but as I heard everyone outside playing. I soon began to take short cuts. I just filled in circles without reading the questions.

Up through the sixth grade, I was always in the upper level of my grade and my individual class. I liked school. The first day of junior high, though, they began to call out the names of students for each class, starting at the upper levels and then working down to the special education kids.

I watched stunned as I saw all of my friends being called and led away by their respective teachers. At first I thought I had not heard my name called, but I waited. Before long, there were not many students left. I saw

CHAPTER 9

that I was among the very last few classes. My heart twisted when I heard my name called. I had been placed into a class that was one step above the special education kids.

Some of the other kids I knew superficially from my grade school, and I could see them looking at me, surprised I was still there. I could see them smiling and whispering about it. This had to be mistake. I figured the teacher would straighten it out, so I ducked my head and walked along with the others.

It was one of the longest days of my life. I was hurt. I was angry. I was embarrassed. I wanted to cry, and I wanted to scream. But I sat quietly and waited.

I didn't get a chance to speak with the teacher alone until lunch time, but she said that she would check for me. She also warned me she might not be able to find out for a day or two as things were very busy for the counselors during the first few days of school. Even as she said this, I could see that she didn't believe me. I could see in her face that she thought I was supposed to be there.

Those two days turned into several months. For a while it seemed as if my parents made daily visits to the school. In the mean time, I was skating through the school work. It required almost no effort. I think I had only one paper or test without a 100 percent. The teacher would congratulate me on my studying, but I wasn't. In fact, I spent most of the day reading and occasionally helping out some of my classmates who were having difficulty. This made the situation a bit more bearable.

The work was just too simple. The one piece of work that I didn't receive 100 percent on during that time was one in which I found a mistake the teacher had missed. When I pointed it out to the teacher, the class whooped and hollered because the paper was not perfect. I remember looking at the teacher, and she smiled. I could see she was a little embarrassed. I didn't know whether she was embarrassed for missing the mistake or for my getting laughed at. I then realized she was not bothering to really go over my work. Even she knew there was no reason to.

I had been sick a lot my first twelve years. Asthma can affect you in so many ways. It's tough to have to sit and watch others play and run. What I was feeling now though was much worse than what I felt when I was sick. Maybe it was because on some level I recognized the asthmatic condition was not my fault, but something I was born with and had to live with. The school situation was a sickness as well, but not physical. Rather, it was like a sickness imposed from the outside upon the heart. I felt more alone and more of an outsider than I had ever felt my entire life.

About halfway through the school year, the school administration said they had made a mistake and were going to move me up one level. They claimed they couldn't move me back in with the students I had always been with because too much time had passed and those classes were "too far ahead." I would never be able to catch up. Years later I would realize that the administration just couldn't admit that such a mistake had been made. Their moving me up one level was a way of demonstrating their sincerity, but it was just an empty gesture. I was caught in between two worlds. I did not fit in my present class, but I couldn't be moved to where I should have been because my former class was too far ahead.

Prior to being moved, I would see the unicorn again. It was a Saturday morning in late fall, after one of the very first heavy frosts. Although much of the woods had been cut for housing, there were still some untouched areas. As I looked out the kitchen window to the back yard, I could see the silvery white coating of frost on the grass and on the trees along the creek. The whole world seemed to have been transformed over night.

I put on my jacket and went out through the garage to the back patio. As I stood there I could see my breath in the cool morning air, and I blew a couple of imaginary smoke rings. I heard the morning dove as I usually did, and then I heard the bobwhite. I whistled back at it, not really expecting a response. I was just excited to hear it because I hadn't heard it in some time.

To my surprise, it answered, and I felt a breeze brush across me. I heard a soft tinkling sound that was familiar, but which I couldn't quite place. I walked down the back yard toward the creek. The grass crackled beneath my feet as my shoes made imprints in the frost. I squatted next to the creek and felt the water. It was cool, but not as cool as I had expected.

As I started to stand, I noticed some prints along the bank. They didn't look like a dog's prints. They were hoof prints, but more heart shaped. I immediately concluded it was a deer, and I decided to follow the tracks. The creek wound past the first section of woods, the backyards of several houses, and into another field before it angled across the road. On the other side of the creek bend were more woods, and past those woods was yet another field with another smaller stream running through it.

As I got to the bend in the creek, the hoof prints picked up on the other side of the creek, leading toward the other woods. No longer was my deer following the creek. I was excited. I felt like a real tracker. The hoof prints were so easy to make out on the frosty ground, I leaped the creek and followed the tracks into the woods with my eyes.

It was then I felt a breeze again, hearing that same strange sound. Again I looked around, searching for the source. The sound quickly faded and so again I ignored it. I followed the tracks through the woods, and as I came out the other side, the tracks ended at the edge of the field. The grass and weeds were waist high or a little taller and they, like everything else, were dipped in frost. But there were no tracks leading into the grass. The tracks just ceased to exist at the edge of the field.

Looking for signs, I walked ten to fifteen yards in both directions. There were no prints, no bent weeds—no sign whatsoever the tracks had ever been there. I retraced my steps to the woods to see if I had missed something. There was nothing! Not even the original tracks! I knew I hadn't imagined them, but there was no sign of any tracks other than my own footprints.

My heart jumped, and I quickly backtracked to the creek. I stood there, stunned. Even the tracks along the creek had disappeared. My eyes searching, I walked back to that field, but there was nothing.

Then a breeze brushed me a third time, again with that soft bell sound. As I looked up and out across the field, I saw this head rise up out of the weeds not fifty yards away. I caught my breath. It stood in the middle of the field, looking at me, and I saw recognition in those eyes.

I remembered the first time I saw those eyes when I was sitting on my sassafras tree next to the pond. The unicorn actually seemed to smile at my remembering. I could see its warm breath in the cool air, and the horn seemed to glisten with frost as well. It held my eyes for the longest time, and before I could blink or move, it turned and in two leaps, disappeared from view.

I ran out to the spot where I had seen it, but there was nothing there. Only weeds, still covered with frost and still standing tall. There was no sign of it at all. No sign that it had ever been there. As I walked back to the house, the frost was melting. I debated telling others what I had seen, but I knew they wouldn't believe.

Over the next week, things began to feel different. The situation at school did not matter nearly as much. There was a quietness, a calm. A kind of acceptance. Part of me knew the situation at school was not going to change in any substantial manner. A part of me knew something would still be gained from the situation even though at the time I had no idea what it would be.

It was around this time my interest in things of the spirit became more serious. The time I would have spent trying to catch up to my class, had I been placed properly, became time spent exploring other realms. I began to read and study about astrology and ghosts and fairies and elves. I began to listen to the birds and began to practice psychic development.

Over time I began to realize this was why the unicorn had returned, but it took many years for this realization to fully register. If the unicorn had not returned when it did, the changes that would have unfolded for me are a little frightening to think about. I would have been led along an entirely different path and perception of the world.

CHAPTER 9

From that moment on, there has always been a part of me that knows I am protected and things will eventually work out the way they are supposed to. The difficulty for me, as for most people, was learning to trust that feeling.

In many ways, the journey through this book has led us back to where we first began. Quests never truly end. Not even for the unicorn. They just go on to new levels. Many may still scoff at the possibility of unicorns and at my own belief in them and other wondrous aspects of life. I can never prove or disprove their existence, and I doubt that I would ever want to try. It is neither my task nor intention to do so. That I leave to others more "rational."

> The question of historicity and actuality with regard to gods and unicorns is a relatively trifling matter which may be left to antiquarians and biologists, for both the god and the unicorn had a business to perform greater than any mere existence in the flesh could explain or provide a basis for.[1]

Dragons, unicorns, and other wondrous beasts are scarce within the natural world and within modern beliefs. With the disappearance of natural lands and wilderness comes the disappearance of many beliefs—even those considered fantastic and mystical. With the loss of natural lands and wilderness also comes a loss of belief in the wonders of the world.

Every year more and more animals become endangered or extinct. Thousands of species are threatened. Millions of acres of natural land are destroyed every year. In the modern world, we have separated the natural world and all of its wonders from ourselves. Nature is something to be studied, examined, or used for personal gain. Too many people assume that destruction of wildlife and habitat has no affect upon them, either

---

[1] Odell Shepherd, *The Lore of the Unicorn* (New York: Avenel Books, 1982), p. xi.

individually or as a society because the affects are not readily apparent. There is so much we don't know about the world we should be careful about destroying aspects which may be beneficial to us in the future, both physically and spiritually. In the Amazon River area alone, 30-50 percent of the plants and animals are still unidentified.

Everything in nature, even those things many may believe are fantastic, serve a purpose. We may not understand that role or purpose, but we should be careful not to dismiss it. Do we truly need to justify the existence of and our belief in a plant, an animal, or even a unicorn any more than we should justify the existence of humans? Our ability or willingness to believe in possibilities should not be based upon a presumed level of intelligence, worth, or productivity. Who among us is qualified to determine such a thing?

People often raise their eyebrows to my approach to life. Should I approach life from such a mystical and fantastic perspective? I think so. You don't have to believe all of the mythology or accept all of the mysticism, but by merely examining it and keeping an open mind, we stir ancient primal parts of our soul, a part of us that can see and experience many wonders.

Sometimes in life it is more important to feel than it is to know. By stirring those ancient embers, by remembering what we felt as a child, we rediscover the joys and mysteries of the world. Most people experience a tremendous lack of wonder in their daily lives. Humans can starve from a lack of wonder as much as from a lack of food.

The unicorn legacy is a reminder. When twin images of the archetypal male and female combine in myth, in images, and in life as the unicorn, we should pay attention. We have in this image a powerful, transforming, life-restoring agent. We have something to help us find what has been lost, heal what has been hurt, and restore life to what has died within us. We rediscover our wonder.

The sacred quest is the path of initiation. The quest for the unicorn, as with all quests, leads down many paths. Each path helps to cut and polish us into a priceless gem. In more ancient times, the spiritual student underwent symbolic faceting. Each phase of training would bring the individual to new wonders hidden within the physical world. The last phase would lead the individual into what was once known as the "Holy of Holies."

The Holy of Holies consisted of an empty chamber. No symbols. No altars. No tools. Just an empty chamber. Here the student was left alone to find the Divine that exists within emptiness. Here the student learned to rely on the higher self and the innate knowledge of the union that exists between all humans and the divine world. Here, in the darkness of the last temple of the sacred quest, only the student can bring light and illumination. Here, only the student can light the lamp that brings brilliance out of darkness. Here, the student ceases to look for a light to shine down, but rather, the student looks for the light within—to shine out.

This is the lesson of the Divine Within, the beginning of the Greater Mysteries. It is then we realize magic and miracles are supposed to happen. We discover life is supposed to work. We find enchanted worlds still exist. And we remember the unicorn which led us here dances forever within our hearts!

> Yet, if you enter the woods
> Of a summer evening late,
> When the night air cool on the trout-ringed pools...
> You will hear the beat of a horse's feet,
> And the swish of a skirt in the dew,
> Steadily cantering through
> The misty solitudes,
> As though they perfectly knew
> The old lost road through the woods...
> But there is no road through the woods.

Rudyard Kipling
"The Way Through the Woods"
Two Ways of Seeing

REFERENCES

Alden, Laura. *Learning About Unicorns.* Chicago, IL: Children's Press, 1985.

Anand, Margol. *The Art of Sexual Ecstasy.* Los Angeles, CA: Jeremy P. Tarcher, 1989.

Andrews, Ted. *Animal-Speak.* St. Paul, MN: Llewellyn Publications, 1993.

_____. *Enchantment of the Faerie Realm.* St. Paul, MN: Llewellyn Publications, 1993.

_____. *Crystal Balls and Crystals Bowls.* St. Paul, MN: Llewellyn Publications, 1995.

_____. *The Occult Christ: Angelic Mysteries and the Divine Feminine.* St. Paul, MN: Llewellyn Publications, 1993.

Anodea, Judith. *Wheels of Life.* St. Paul, MN: Llewellyn Publications, 1988.

Auden, W.H. *Collected Short Poems.*

Aylesworth, Thomas. *The Alchemists: Magic into Science.* Reading, MA: Addison-Wesley, 1973.

Barbault, Armand. *Gold of a Thousand Mornings.* London: Neville Spearman, 1969.

Barber, Richard and Richer, Anne. *Dictionary of Fabulous Beasts.* London: Macmillan, 1971.

Baring-Gold, Sabine. *Curious Myths of the Middle Ages.* London: Longmans, Green & Co., 1906.

Beagle, Peter S. The Last Unicorn. New York: Viking Press, 1968.

Bedingfeld, Henry and Peter Gwynn-Jones. Heraldry. Secaucus, NJ: Chartwell Books, 1993.

Brown, Robert. *The Unicorn: Mythological Investigation.* London: Longmans, 1881.

Cameron, Julia. *The Artist's Way.*

Campbell, Joseph. *The Hero with a Thousand Faces.* Princeton, NJ: Princeton University Press, 1949.

Carroll, Lewis. *Through the Looking Glass.*

Chaney, Robert. *Transmutation: How the Alchemists Turned Lead into Gold.* Upland: Astara, 1969.

Chang, Stephen T. *The Tao of Sexology.* San Francisco, CA: Tao Publishing, 1986.

_____. *The Complete System of Self-Healing.* San Francisco, CA: Tao Publishing, 1986.

Clark, Anne. *Beasts and Bawdy: A Book of Fabulous & Fantastic Beasts.* New York: Taplinger Publications, 1975.

Costello, Peter. *The Magic Zoo: Natural History of Fabulous Animals.* New York: St. Martin's Press; 1979.

Coville, Bruce, ed. *The Unicorn Treasury*. New York: Doubleday, 1988.

De Bingen, Hildegarde. *Physica*.

Demi. *Demi's Dragons and Fantastic Creatures*. New York: Henry Holt and Company.

Douglas, Nik and Slinger, Penny. *Sexual Secrets*. New York: Destiny Books, 1979.

Eberhard, Wolfram. *A Dictionary of Chinese Symbols*. London: Routledge, 1986.

Finneran, Richard J., ed. *Collected Poems of W.B. Yeats*. New York: Macmillan Publishing Co., 1989.

Frazer, Sir James G. *Folklore in the Old Testament*. New York: Avenel Books, 1988.

Freeman, Margaret B. *The Unicorn Tapestries*. New York: Metropolitan Museum of Art, 1979.

Giblin, James Cross. *The Truth About Unicorns*. New York: Harper Collins, 1991.

Godwin, Malcolm. *The Holy Grail*. New York: Viking Press, 1994.

Hall, Manly P. *Paracelsus*. Los Angeles, CA: Philosophical Research Society, 1964.

Hathaway, Nancy. *The Unicorn*. New York: Viking Press, 1980.

Jung, Carl. *Psychology and Alchemy*. Princeton, NJ: Princeton University Press, 1953.

Junius, Manfred. *Practical Handbook of Plant Alchemy*. New York: Inner Traditions International, 1985.

Khanna, Madha. *Yantra*. London: Thames and Hudson, 1979.

Kipling, Rudyard. *Two Ways of Seeing*.

Land, J.P.N., ed./trans. *Anecdota Syriaca*. Strassburg: Lugd Batav, 1870.

Lucien, Francis. *Allegories*.

Lum, Peter. *Fabulous Beasts*. New York: Pantheon Books, 1951.

McGaa, Ed. *Mother Earth Spirituality*. San Francisco, CA: Harper, 1990.

McHargue, Georgess. *The Beasts of Never*. New York: Bobbs-Merrill Company, 1968.

Ming, Yang Jwing. *Northern Shaolin Sword*. Jamaica Plain: YMAA Publications, 1992

Mao, Li and Wu, Zong. *Ancient Way to Keep Fit*. Bolinas: Shelter Publications, 1992.

Moulton, LeArta A. *Herb Walk*. Provo, UT: Gluten Co., Inc., 1979.

Palmer, Robin. *Dragons, Unicorns and Other Magical Beasts*. New York: Henry Walck, Inc., 1966.

Paterson, Helena. *Handbook of Celtic Astrology*. St. Paul, MN: Llewellyn Publications, 1994.

Poltarnees, Welleran. *A Book of Unicorns*. La Jolla, CA: Green Tiger Press, 1978.

REFERENCES

Pratt, Davis and Kula, Elsa. *Magic Animals of Japan*. Berkeley, CA: Parnassus Press, 1967.

Regardie, Israel. *The Complete Golden Dawn System of Magic*. Phoenix, AZ: Falcon Press, 1984.

Schrader, J.L. *A Medieval Bestiary*. New York: Metropolitan Museum of Art, 1986.

Shepard, Odell. *The Lore of the Unicorn*. New York: Avenel Books, 1982.

Stewart, R.J. *The Underworld Invitation*. Northamptonshire: Aquarian Press, 1985.

Vavra, Robert. *Unicorns I Have Known*. New York: William Morrow and Company, Inc., 1983.

Waite, Arthur E., trans. *The Coelum Philosophorun By Paracelsus*. London: Evanescent Press;, 1894.

White, T.H. *The Bestiary: A Book of Beasts*. New York: G.P. Putnam's Sons, 1953.

Williams, Tennessee. *The Glass Menagerie*.

INDEX

A

Adam 143
Aelian 13
African unicorn 83
alchemical mysteries 190
alchemists 192
alchemy 52, 153, 191
Alexander the Great 13, 84, 145
alicorn 30, 47
alicorn's symbolism
   luminosity 55
   shape 51
   spirals 53
ancient Persia 77
Anecdota Syriaca 142
animal totem 123
antelope 83
antlers 51
apple 34
apple blossom 67
Arabia 77, 83
archangels
   See Auriel
   See Michael
   See Gabriel
archetypal energies 130
archetypal symbols 50, 152
archetype 8, 24
Argus of a Hundred Eyes 174
Arien age 145
astrology 62
athame 59
Auden, W.H. 27
auric vision 51
Auriel 56, 153
autumn 30, 35

B

Babylonia 106
Bartholomew 30, 120
basil 166
bestiaries of the world 14

Bible references 145
birds 37
blazon 124
Book of Isaiah 145, 147
Book of Job 147
Books of Psalms 147
bowls 152
brow chakra 51, 151
Bucephalus 13, 84
Buddha
   hymn of 76
butterflies 36, 38, 175

C

Caesar 13
Canadian border 13
Cancer 120
Capricorn 152
Carroll, Lewis 10
cauldrons 152
cedar 67
cedar trees 34
Celtic calendar 62
Celtic lunar astrology 35
Celtic mythology 62
Celtic tradition 28, 35
Centaury 36
Chaldean checkerboard 106
charges 124
Charles VI 48, 108
Ch'i Lin 77, 79, 81, 82, 101
chicory 36
China 12–15, 77, 168
Chinese 170
Chinese creation myth 77, 164
Christ 147
Christian 13
Christian mystics 151
Christianity 169
cinnamon 135
circle 53, 126

Closing Scenario 74
clover 35, 67
Coats of Arms 107, 122
collective unconscious 25
color therapy 57
Confucius 12, 81
cornucopia 152
Council of Imaginary Beasts 92
creative principle 52
crescent 126
cross 126
Ctesius 13, 47
cup 152

D

damselfly 31
Dances of the Sacred Beasts 86
Daniel 143
Dapper, Dr. Olfert 13
dark warrior 170
David 143, 146
deer 36, 153, 176
dexter 124
diamond 126
dinosaur unicorn 11
DNA molecule 207
DNA spiral 54
Douglas, Nik 190
doves 36, 173
dragon
    56, 59, 77, 78, 164, 166, 192
dragon force 56
Dragon Gates 167
dragon pose 88
dragonfly 31, 166, 177
dragonslayer 56
    See also Michael
dreams 123
Durer, Albrecht 205
Dweller on the Threshold 56, 201

E

Eastern Unicorn 76, 79
Effigy Song 80
Egypt 38, 174
elements 216
elephant 83
Elixir of Life 191
Elizabeth I 106
empathy 218
encounter cautions 44
encounter guidelines 44
England 13, 106
eroticism 210
esoteric Christianity 56, 120

F

Facing the Shadow Self 201
Faerie Realm 23, 27, 34, 153, 205
falcon 171
feathers 175
fertility 32
field 124
firefly 166
Florida 13
flower elixirs 67
flute 222
fragrances 67
Fu Hsi 82, 170

G

Gabriel 144
Garden of Eden 143
gem elixirs 67
Genghis Khan 81
gentleness 32
German folk song 105
Germany 13
Genghis Khan and the Unicorn 100
giraffe 83
goddesses
    Diane 203
    Hera 174

golden eagle 171
grail cup 152
grail legends 56
Greek 13
griffin 171
guardians of the forest 164
guru 54
Gwynvyd 62, 63

H

hawk 166
healing 33
healing aspect 52
healing techniques 80
hearing 178
heat lightning 172
Henry II of France 48
heraldic charges 125
heraldic colors 125
heraldic shield illustration 123
heraldry 106, 123
higher self 200
Hildegarde de Bingen 47, 149
Hindu holy man 182
holly 34
Holly month 62
holly spirit 35
Holy Child 33, 53, 62, 205
Holy Grail 23, 132, 147, 193
Holy of Holies 234
Holy Quest 169
  purpose of 152
horn of plenty 152
horn of salvation 151
horse 53, 83
horse cults 62
horse dragon 170
horse goddess 62
horse stance 59-60
horses 36
Huang Ti 81

humans 107
hummingbirds 36, 173

I

I Ching 82, 170
Ibis 38, 175
imaginary beasts 92
imagination 49
incenses 67
India 12, 100
initiation 53, 194
innocence 52
Iran 77
Iraq 77
Isabel 119
Iskandar
  See Alexander the Great

J

Japan 77
Japanese 177
Jesus 56, 153
Job 143
John of Hesse 47
journaling
  benefits of 18
  guidelines 20
Julius Caesar 13
Jung, Carl 25

K

Karkadann 12–15, 77, 83
Kasyapa 182
Katya and the Unicorn story 70
K'i Lin 77
  See also Ch'i Lin
King Edward I 48
King John II 13
King Nebuchadnezzar 144
Kipling, Rudyard 234
Kirin 77, 80
knife 59

knight 119
Knight of the Lion 120
  See also Bartholomew
Korea 77
kundalini 54, 207, 208

L

Lammas 35
lavender 67
law of the flaming sword 56
libido 84
lightning 172
lilac 34, 67
lily family 36
lion 80, 105, 119
lioness 80
lizard 166
longevity 215
Luini, Bernardino 203

M

Madonna 205
magic wand 52
magickal dance 58, 59
magickal rituals 59
magickal storytelling 66
  Closing Scenario 74
  guidelines for 67
  Opening Scenario 68
Mahabharata, The 12, 180
Maine 13
mandala 124
maple syrup 34
Marco Polo 13
martial arts forms 80
Mary, Queen of Scots 48, 106
meadows 34, 172, 176
medicine 122
medicine shields 122, 123
Medieval Fighting Unicorn 107
meditations 93
mercury 192

Michael 56, 153
Middle Ages 13, 47, 82, 106
Middle East 77
Middle Eastern unicorn 83
monoceros 143
monoclonius 11
morality 149
musky 169
Mycenean coins 106
myrrh 168
mystic marriage 33

N

narwal 48
Nathaniel.
  See Bartholomew
Native Americans 122, 126, 170, 177
Nephele 203
nervous system 215
Nigeria 170
nightingale 36
Noah 143
nuthatches 36

O

Oak month 62
oils 67
Old Testament 145
Opening Scenario 68
orchid 67
oryx 11

P

paintings 148
peacock 36, 38, 168, 174
Pentateuch 147
perception 218
Persephone 151, 205
Persia 12, 83
pheasant 168, 174
Phillip II of Spain 48
Philosopher's Stone 191

INDEX

phoenix 30, 38, 59, 77, 78, 164-168
phoenix myth 30
phoenix pose 89
Physiologus 13, 149
Piscean age 145
places, best
   to encounter unicorns 42
Pliny 13
Pluto 149, 205
Pope Clement 48
pregnancy 216
primitive humans 107
primitive peoples 130
Procris 203
prophecy of paradox 8
Pulci, Luca 203
purity 32, 52

Q
Quest for the Holy Grail 152

R
Ragged John 16, 194
Rainbow River 62
ram 144
Rape of Persephone 205
rebirth 52, 200
red clover 35
redemption 197
regeneration 195
Renaissance 13, 47
renewal 195
Rhiannon 62
rhinoceros 48
Roc 84
Roman 13
Royal Arms of Great Britain 106
Royal Arms of Scotland 106
Russian folktale 70

S
sacred beasts 77, 210
Sacred Loop 123
sacred marriage 192, 194, 205
sacred path 198
sacred quest 195
sacred sex 210
sacred sexuality 202
salamander 166
salvation 197
Sanskrit 180
Satan 147
Scotland 13, 106
Scottish unicorn 106
season of rut 30
Septuagint 143
serpent 147
sexual energy 52, 207
sexual positions
   phoenix 214
   tortoise 214
   turning dragon 214
   unicorn 214
sexuality 32
sexually abused children 52
Shaktipat 55
shamanic shield symbols 126
shamans 58, 130
Shaolin Long-Fist Sword 59
shapeshifting 180
shields 122
signs of dragons 167
Sin-you 77, 80
sinister 124
six-rayed star 126
Slinger, Penny 190
smell 178
snake 166
snapdragon 67
soul retrieval 198

spice 135
spiral dances 53
spirals 53
spring 106
square 126
St. Luke 151
stag 83
stamina 215
sugar maple 34
summer 106
sword 56, 153
symbol 59, 105, 146
    feminine 53, 152
Syriaca 142

T

talisman 124
Talmud 143
Tantra 207
Tantrism 207
Taoism 80, 207
Taoist 210
Taoist healing position 215
Test of Discrimination 196
Test of the Teacher 201
Test of Uncontrolled Fancy 198
therapy 57
Thibaut 202
third eye 51, 151
thunder 172
tiger 80
tonic meditation 92
tortoise 77, 78, 164, 169
tortoise pose 90
tortoise shell 170
totems 123
transformation 33, 193, 195
triangle 126
trust in the higher self 200
turtle 169, 178
    See also tortoise

U

uncontrolled fancy 198
    unicorn 11, 59, 70, 77, 78
gifts of 29
unicorn encounter 43-46
unicorn folk song 105
unicorn root 36
unicorn stance 28, 59, 61
unicornis 143
Unicorn's Companions 162

V

Vietnam 77, 80
violet 67
virgin 108, 149
visions 123
vulture 171

W

wands 52
water conning 47
Welsh mythology 62
white hart 28
wild honey 34
Williams, Tennessee 226
wood nymph 218
woodland being 218
woodpeckers 36

Y

yang 80
yantra 53, 124
Yen Ching-tsai 81
Yellow Emperor 81
yin 80

ABOUT THE AUTHOR

Ted Andrews is an internationally recognized author, storyteller, teacher, and mystic. A leader in the human potential and metaphysical fields, his books have been translated into nine foreign languages, and he is often featured on both national and local television and radio programs.

A teacher and counselor for ten years, Ted has an extensive formal and informal education in teaching, and has the ability to make the esoteric practical and accessible to everyone.

Called a true Renaissance man, Ted is schooled in music and healing, and he is a continuing student of the ballet and kung fu. He holds state and federal permits to work with his own birds of prey, and he conducts animal education and storytelling programs throughout the United States.

ABOUT THE ILLUSTRATOR

Pat Hart operates her own art studio and has taught art privately for 20 years. She is recognized for her authentic, historical, and mythical detail. Pat is an art visionary of the heart and mind, and her reputation for fantasy work that stirs the soul has grown from the Texas Renaissance galleries to an ever-widening national audience.

Prints of the cover art for *Treasures of the Unicorn*, along with other unicorn illustrations and fantasy works by Pat Hart may be obtained through: Hart to Heart Originals, 4608 Davis Hall Road, Santa Fe, TX, (409) 925-6665

ABOUT THE BOOK DESIGNER AND EDITOR

Diane Haugen and **Pagyn Alexander-Harding** take manuscripts from draft form to camera-ready copy, including editing and indexing. They specialize in working with authors to design page layouts to enhance content, increase reader understanding, and create books inviting to the eye. They may be reached at IAAI, Hitterdal, MN, 56552, (218) 962-3202. URL: http://www.infoauto.com.